T0065688

WHEN

THE

SMILES

CEASE

PRESLEY SAINT-CYR

WESTBOW
PRESS®
A DIVISION OF THOMAS NELSON
& ZONDERVAN

WestBow Press books may be ordered through booksellers or by contacting:

WestBow Press
A Division of Thomas Nelson & Zondervan
1663 Liberty Drive
Bloomington, IN 47403
www.westbowpress.com
844-714-3454

ISBN: 978-1-6642-9334-2 (sc)
ISBN: 978-1-6642-9335-9 (hc)
ISBN: 978-1-6642-9333-5 (e)

Library of Congress Control Number: 2023903211

Print information available on the last page.

WestBow Press rev. date: 02/23/2023

Vanity of vanities, all is vanity.
—King Solomon

CONTENTS

CHAPTER 1

THE LONG GOODBYE

Paul would never forget the days he spent with his father. In particular, he recalled the times when he and his father ventured to school on their motorcycle. He vividly remembered the farewells and the smiles. There were times when their discussions lacked discretion. Paul knew he was blessed to be part of a structured family such as his; he was loved and accepted. Now, the time had come to leave his beloved father and immigrate to an unknown country.

"Paul!" Margaret called out. "It's time for you to get up and get ready. The plane leaves in two hours."

"Yes, Mother," Paul replied.

He had been anticipating this great day—a day when life would become completely different from how he had known it. He wondered what it would be like to leave his father, as well as his relatives, and it dawned on him—*Who will I discuss my school issues with? How will I overcome my grief from our separation?*

He mustered all his strength and took his clothes off the hanger. He inspected them one last time and then got dressed. He took his white sneakers from their box and slipped his feet into them. He tied the laces with the little strength he had left and withdrew his luggage from the corner of the room. "Mom, I am ready now. Are we all ready to depart?"

"Wait, darling. I am almost finished dressing your sister," she said calmly.

He went to the living room and noticed that his uncle was sitting with a plate of food as he waited. "Uncle Charles, how much more time do we have?" Paul asked.

"Don't worry, son. We have about two hours before the plane leaves."

Mr. Charles was Paul's godfather as well as his most beloved uncle. Paul often discussed important matters with his uncle and trusted every word he said.

Paul paced around the room, wondering where his father was. He was supposed to escort them to the airport, but Paul had yet to see him. "Uncle Charles, may I borrow your phone please?" Paul asked.

"Here, son," said his uncle.

Paul dialed the number and waited.

And waited.

Just before he gave up, he heard the voice of the man who had never let him down. His joy rose like the sunrise. "Dad, how are you? I miss you. We're waiting for you and are wondering if everything is all right," Paul said with a quivering voice.

"I am all right, son. Due to the intense traffic, the trip has taken longer than expected. Come to the gate in five minutes. I am almost there," said his dad.

Paul informed his uncle of the news and thought once again of the separation.

If only the circumstances of life had not necessitated their emigration. He thought about his dad, Antoine, a well-known college professor, and his mom, Margaret, a teacher of the elementary grades. Despite their socioeconomic status, the unfair system in Haiti would put their children at a disadvantage. There were prodigies who remained jobless in Haiti because there weren't any opportunities for them to flourish. Academia, which was the hope of many, left many in anguish, as the country lacked the right departments to give them the necessary jobs. This fact was apparent to Margaret, Antoine, and Paul. The parents knew that the American dream would empower their children to become the best they could be. If they were going to make a strong impact in the world, emigrating from Haiti had to be their course of action.

After everyone was ready, Paul went to the gate to greet his dad. He noticed his dad's look of despair. Paul understood that his dad would be very unhappy for quite some time. He clutched his dad with his arms and welcomed him. Margaret came outside with one suitcase and kissed her husband. Antoine assisted her with the remaining valise, and everyone got in the car. Antoine asked if everyone was seated, and Paul responded, "We're all here."

After receiving the confirmation, Uncle Charles fired up the engine of his car and pulled out of the driveway. The long journey, which had already begun in Paul's mind, now became real.

About thirty minutes later, the family arrived at the Port-au-Prince airport.

The airport was crowded, as usual. The man in blue attire at the grand entrance made sure that everyone entered safely. The main inspection had not yet begun, but Paul knew that it was coming.

They moved along, and everyone took his or her luggage. Paul noticed the diverse groups of people at the airport. He had never seen so many white individuals; he was quite amazed. When Paul turned around, he saw Margaret and Antoine staring into each other's eyes. He could see tears welling in their eyes. His parents exchanged words that did not reach Paul's ears. They were very standing close to Paul, but somehow, it was like sound had lost its power to be transmitted through the air.

His father and mother gave their last farewells to each other in their own way. Paul hugged his father one last time and went to the waiting area. He had come to the realization that he would be the head of the household now. His father's absence meant that Paul would be more involved in helping his mom and his sister.

An announcement was made for final boarding, and Paul and his mom and sister got in line for the flight to Florida. From where he stood, Paul could see the massive airplanes awaiting departure.

The flight attendant verified their identification and told them they were cleared to board the plane.

Paul felt relieved and ecstatic. "Mom, this is it!"

"Yes, my son," she answered, "the time has come for us to start a new life. We soon will know what it is like to dwell in a developed country. The world undoubtedly will be different from how we knew it."

When they boarded the plane, Paul saw a flight attendant helping everyone to their seats. It seemed that many people, like him, had never been on a plane before. He, too, needed help. "Excuse me, madam. Do you know where seat 24A is?" he asked.

"Come with me," the flight attendant replied. About twenty rows down, she pointed to their seats.

Paul looked carefully and saw the numbers above the seats. He sat down and felt the comfort of the seat. He wondered again about this new life, this grand departure.

Not long thereafter, a woman sat down on his right.

"Hello," he said. It was the only English word he knew.

It must have been obvious to the woman that English was not Paul's first language because she said in Creole, "How are you?"

"I am doing well. Thank you," responded Paul. He told her that this was his first time on a plane—he had many questions. They then had a conversation about America.

"My friend, if you stay focused in that country, you will achieve everything you desire," she said.

"What is your name?" Paul asked.

"My name is Martha."

Paul thought about that name. He had not known any other Haitian named Martha. "I am Paul," he said in return.

"Nice to meet you, Paul," Martha said with an amiable smile.

After that, they were silent for the rest of the flight. Paul wanted to take in the flying experience. He did not want to delve into deep conversations. Soon, he fell into a very peaceful sleep.

When the plane arrived, and Paul and his mom and sister followed the other passengers exiting the plane. He saw many great lights. He had never been in a place so technologically advanced. He felt as if great opportunities awaited. They then went into a very long line. It was not much different from what he had experienced in Haiti, but now, the anticipation was much greater.

At last, their documents were checked, and they exited the airport.

From a distance, Paul could see his uncle in his white SUV. "Mom, I see Uncle Mark," he cried jubilantly.

"I believe it's him," confirmed Margaret.

Uncle Mark took the suitcases and set them in the trunk of the car. His movements were swift.

It had been a year since Paul had last seen him. Paul always felt great respect for Uncle Mark. He had helped his father financially when he needed it the most. Two years ago, when he was just 7 years old, Paul's father brought Paul to the bank to get the money that Mark had sent. Although the aid was not critical, it was nevertheless helpful in the completion of his father's house. Everyone from his father's side took great pride in it.

CHAPTER 2

THE GREAT DEPARTURE

Antoine saw the beautiful sunset as he glanced at the sky. His wife, Margaret, and his two children had just departed to go to an unfamiliar country. He felt his heart was being torn apart. There were other particular sensations that he could not shake off—anxiety, agony, anguish; these were the emotions that anyone who loved others would feel in such situation. He already perceived the many days when he would not see his wife's beautiful face. He also imagined the many days when he would not take Paul to school on his motorcycle or see the joy on his son's face. As a father who took care of his house, he already realized the many hugs he would be deprived of. Now, those moments would be only memories. He took his handkerchief and wiped his face. He then blew his nose and tried to conjure optimistic thoughts. He wanted to cry, but his maturity would not permit it. He understood that, as part of being a man, he had to be strong. He never really understood why, but that's what he was taught.

"Hey, sir, the bus is about to leave. Do you have your fare?"

"Yes," he answered. As he sat on the bus, a stream of tears began to flow. *If only*, he thought, *if only this was not necessary*. He thought of his extended family, the ones who'd been there for him since the beginning. He thought about his profession and the joy that it had brought him—the things that gave his life meaning. As the bus drove through the village, he noticed the farmers tilling the land. He saw the crops that had died as a result of the rain shortage in the last few months.

Across from him was a portable radio, tuned to the news. "Two passenger busses were found abandoned at 10:00 p.m.," the announcer said. "Investigators are using all of their resources to find the victims of what they believe was a hijacking. Please stay tuned for more updates on Radio Metropol."

As Antoine arrived at the Gonaives station, he felt a sense of relief and gratefulness. These days, security was quite an issue. He fastened his backpack on him and exited the bus. He pulled out his phone and dialed Barius. "Hey, brother, where are you?"

"I'm here, Antoine. I'm near Ms. Maggie's store."

"OK, I am coming." He looked to his right and his left to orient himself. He could see Frank's corner store; he knew that Maggie's machinery store was three stores adjacent to it. He rapidly crossed the street and could see Barius's car in the distance.

Antoine entered the store and saw his brother. "Barius!" he shouted.

"Antoine, my brother, how was the trip?"

"It was all right."

"I wish I had taken you, but these days, our lives are too important to risk it. Being in a bus with many other people increases one's chance of survival. Suppose something were to go wrong," said Barius.

"I understand, brother," Antoine said. He knew that people who drove by themselves were more likely to get hijacked. He took his wallet from his purse and looked at the photo of his family again.

"Don't worry, Antoine. Everything will be all right," Barius reassured him. "Remember, you have us. We will assist you in anything you may need. We are here for you."

When they arrived at Antoine's house, he saw his niece Syndie standing by the doorway. She appeared to have been waiting for them in desperation. She came to meet them at the gate with a sigh of relief. She hugged both of them as if she had longed for them for her entire life.

"How's everyone doing, Syndie?" Antoine asked as they walked back to the house.

"Everyone's fine, Uncle Antoine."

He opened the door and saw many faces that he had not seen for the past day. After greeting everyone, he went straight to his room.

He noticed that his bed was nicely made, and the room had a very welcoming scent. Adjacent to his room was Paul's room, and next to that was his sister Ransel's room. Opposite Ransel's room was his sister Julian's room, which she shared with one of her children. Because of Uncle's Mark contribution to the house, Antoine felt that his sisters had a right to live there. He loved their presence, but he knew that Margaret found it despicable. Margaret would have preferred living with just her family.

With Margaret gone now, though, Antoine knew that Julian and Ransel, as well as their children, would make his home a sanctuary. Although they both had other options, they were widows, and Antoine had taken it upon himself to help them financially whenever possible. He paid their children's tuition because he believed in education; more importantly, he wanted to uplift the name of his family to those in society. Although he was the second youngest, he was highly revered by his family, and he took great pride in it. All important matters were discussed with him—his education merited it, and greater still, his social status warranted it. He knew his family would greatly appreciate Margaret's absence. This way, they would have Antoine all to themselves.

CHAPTER 3

THE LONGING EFFECT

Paul sat directly across Margaret in their family living room. After they arrived in America, Grandpa had taken the initiative of supporting them for the time being.

"Paul," Margaret said, "the time has come for us to consider what will become of our lives. As you can see, America is quite capitalistic. I don't yet have a job, but I don't know how much longer Grandpa Pradere will be able to support us. It is my responsibility to take care of you and your sister."

"Yes, Mother, I understand."

There were times when Paul felt that his grandfather's home was not suitable for him. Many arguments occurred among the family members, and Paul did not know whether he could bear it any longer. The arguments all seemed to stem from financial disputes. No one tried to understand each other. Those who had stable jobs did not want to help out with the expenses. They did not feel that they were responsible for that.

Every other morning, someone would say something slick, and then another person would join in, and before you knew it, everyone would be shouting at each other.

Paul decided to isolate himself from his relatives whenever possible. When he couldn't, he always was submissive in any contention that arose.

Paul stepped out onto the balcony. From where he stood, he could see the many cars passing by, each with a particular destination. He wondered, *What is my destination? What is my purpose?* He thought of questions, both abstract and concrete, that his young mind could not truly grasp. *Oh,*

Father, if only you were here right now, we would have an enjoyable moment. Perhaps your presence would have been the key in helping me to find my way.

His father, however, was nowhere nearby; he was in Haiti.

One day, after Paul had finished eating his lunch, he heard his mom calling, "Paul, your father is on the phone."

"I am coming, Mother," Paul answered. It was as if his mom knew that he was missing his father's love.

As Margaret handed the phone to Paul, a sense of joy surged through his veins; this was his grandest desire. "Hey, Dad, how are you?" Paul earnestly inquired.

"I am doing quite well, my son."

"I miss you, Dad. I am very sad by your absence."

"I miss you too, son. How are you?"

"I am hanging in there. I'm sure life would be so much better if you were here with us. There is an emptiness in my heart that I cannot seem to fill. I'm sure that it's you I am longing for. If only … if only you were here," Paul said softly. As he uttered the words, the emotions that he had fought to control overtook him. Tears spilled down his cheeks, and he turned his face away to avoid eye contact with his mom. He could not let her see him this way.

With a shaky voice, Antoine replied, "Don't cry, my son. Never forget that I will always love you, and I know you feel the same way,"

Paul gave the phone to his mom and ran toward her room. He plunged his face into the soft creases of the pillow. He felt a slight sense of comfort, but he knew it was temporary. He tried to shake the thoughts from his mind and attended to his homework.

On the following day, Paul came home to find all of his possessions nicely packed. The time had come for them to finally move; there were simply too many arguments.

"Mom, where are we going?"

"We must leave, son. There's too much feuding in this house." Margaret withdrew her phone from her handbag and dialed Antoine's number. Once she had dialed, she felt a sense of tranquility, for she knew someone she deeply loved would answer on the other end. This time she called not to report sorrow or despair but to inquire about the status of Antoine's immigration papers.

"Margaret, how are you and the kids?" Antoine asked.

"They're splendid. Have you received your immigration papers?"

"No, there's a fee that I must pay before all the papers are in order. From where I am right now, I can definitely say that everything is almost ready. By next month, everything should be in order."

"Glory to God!" Margaret screamed. She felt as if the world had been lifted off her shoulders. The many responsibilities she'd had over the years would now be shared. The many days when she would wonder what tomorrow would bring were over; that would no longer be a worry. She recalled the days when tears would not cease to flow from her eyes as she thought about her sorrows. She recalled the many days when her meal for tomorrow was not guaranteed. She remembered the days when her labor would deprive her of all her energy.

She was thankful indeed. She was a good church woman, and at that very moment, she thought of the many ways she would praise God for finally answering her prayers. She thought of committing an act of gratefulness. She planned to stand in the middle of the congregation and praise the Lord for this great thing He had done in her life.

"Keep praying, Antoine," Margaret finally said. She touched the end-call button and gave one last cry of joy. "Paul! Paul, your dad is coming soon!"

Paul could hardly believe it. He'd known that day would eventually come, but he had not known how rapidly that time was approaching.

CHAPTER 4

THE REUNION

"Julian, Barius, everyone, please come. I have some great news to share with you," Antoine shouted as he came through the door of his lovely house. He already missed the house, although he had not yet departed from it. He thought of the countless days when he would open the metal doors and go to the universities to teach. On many days when he returned home, his extended family was waiting for him. Now, the time that he had waited for had finally come.

As his family gathered around him, Antoine could see the excitement on their faces. They had known that he eventually would emigrate, and so they were delighted for him, but his absence would definitely cause instability.

"I am happy to announce that I have been approved and granted a visa to go to America," Antoine said. "I will leave this Friday."

"I am very happy for you, my brother," Barius said, while tears streamed from his eyes.

Antoine believed that his family was happy for him, but beyond that happiness was a deep sorrow. The brother on whom they had counted for so many years would no longer be with them. At that moment, Antoine began to empathize with them and to feel what they were feeling.

"Now it's going to be you with Margaret and the kids," Julian said softly.

"Yes, I will reunite with them. After all, it has been more than four years since I've seen my children. Margaret has longed for me for quite some time. I must go and ease her sorrow. It's the best decision for all of us."

"I know, Antoine, just don't forget us," Ransel said, gripping Antoine's arms.

"He won't," Julian said with a slight smirk.

Antoine did not make much of it. He wondered if this was due to the bond that he had formed with each member of his family. He knew his family loved him and would support all of his decisions. To that point, he had been the sole decision-maker for the entire family. He felt that his family counted on him, trusted him, and loved him genuinely.

Antoine sighed. "I suppose this is it. I won't be with you any longer in the near future." He hugged each one individually and exchanged some loving words with each of them. Thereafter, he went to his room, and listened to the evening news, as usual, and fell fast asleep.

⤐

CHAPTER 5

THE RESOLUTION

Julian could hardly fall asleep after she heard the news. Her only dependable brother was about to leave her. She closed her eyes but then opened them again. She couldn't sleep because she was deeply troubled, too troubled to explain in words the feeling that radiated through her body. She moaned in agony, but moaning could not relieve her pain. She shivered slightly at the thought of Antoine's departure.

Perhaps her greatest sorrow was due to Margaret's reuniting with Antoine. Julian had a profound resentment for Margaret, who was too modest to suit Julian. Antoine's house was under Margaret's name, and Margaret objected to many of the requests Julian made to Antoine. Now the woman she sincerely despised would be in total control of her brother. At that very moment, she thought, *Perhaps I could get rid of Margaret. If she's out of the picture, Antoine would be home, and we would be the possessors of everything he owns.*

There was only one way she could do that without much suspicion: bewitchment.

Suppose Margaret was afflicted with cancer, Julian thought. *Then everyone would assume her death was by natural causes, and Antoine would truly be ours.* She dwelled on that thought throughout the night. *Oh, my,* she thought. *This is quite genius indeed.*

The next day, she took some money from the purse she kept hidden under her bed and headed to Barius's house, where she knocked on the door with great elation.

When Barius opened the door, he looked dreadful look, and Julian could tell that he had been weeping throughout the night.

17

"Barius, my brother, you don't have to be despondent. I have a resolution for our sorrow. We both have a great resentment for Margaret. Ever since Antoine got married, that woman has been an obstacle for all of us. She objects to many of our requests, and I believe the time has come for us to end her."

"But what about her children?" Barius asked. "Who will care for them?"

"Forget about her children. The question is, what about *our* children? Who's going to ensure that they go to school and receive everything they desire. You know that before long, we will lose all of our rights over Antoine's possessions."

"I suppose you're right. What do you suggest?"

"We will ask a witch doctor to give us a potion that will not kill Antoine but that will give Margaret cancer after they come into intimate contact. We also will request that Antoine's love for his wife and children diminish so that his focus will be on us while he's in America."

"Very well," Barius consented.

They were determined to carry out their decision and were absolutely certain that all of the family members would agree. They were doing this for their well-being and for their family name.

Julian anxiously waited for Barius to get ready for the journey. She was familiar with a witch doctor who was quite effective in his sorcery. Because Antoine was not very spiritual, she knew that her desires would be swiftly conducted. As she and Barius walked toward the transportation station, she stayed quiet, contemplating the pain and sorrow Margaret would feel.

At the station, she saw different cars transporting people out of the city. She walked rather quickly, avoiding many, as she tried to reach an automobile that would transport her to her destination.

"Where do you wish to go?" inquired one of the drivers.

"Dupadoo," she answered, trying to hide her glee. She allowed Barius to get in the car first, just in case he considered withdrawing from the mission at the last minute.

It had been a while since Julian had visited the witch doctor. As she gazed out the window, she noticed they were near his small house, a place she loved to visit when she wanted quick results. She knew it was wrong, but she didn't care. She was a woman without emotions; she did whatever she felt was necessary. "Pull over," she told the driver. "We've arrived."

She walked to the door, showed her sign of respect, and gave her request to the witch doctor.

"That will be ten thousand gourdes," said the witch doctor.

"That is all right," Julian agreed. "This matter is very important to us and must be resolved."

The witch doctor then gave her a vial that contained a scarlet liquid; it had a bloody appearance. She didn't know what it was, but she accepted it without any signs of reluctance or doubt. She knew this was necessary.

She and Barius took a bus home and arrived there half an hour later.

She approached Syndie and whispered, "I have a request. I want you to put this in Antoine's drink when he's unaware."

"What is this?" Syndie asked.

"Don't worry about that, child. It won't hurt him. Just do as I say, and be discreet," Julian said.

As the family gathered for their last dinner, Syndie unobtrusively went into the kitchen. She didn't know what she was about to put in the drink, but she trusted her aunt and refused to believe that it was poisonous. Her conscience wanted her to object, but she had already agreed. If anyone ever questioned her, she would have the support of Aunt Julian—she took consolation in that. Syndie served everyone their drinks and made sure that Antoine received the correct one. She had added extra sugar in case the drink had a bitter taste.

Everyone sat together a final time and ate supper. At the conclusion of the meal, Julian watched Antoine lift his cup and drink his juice. She could tell by the way he looked that he was pleased.

"Thank you, Syndie," Antoine said with an approving smile. "That was one of the best drinks I've ever had."

"You're welcome, Uncle. I give the best things to my favorite uncle."

"I suppose you're right." Antoine chuckled, but he felt honored. To be considered as Syndie's favorite uncle meant a lot to him. After all, he had worked for it. He always made sure Syndie's school tuition was paid on time. That was not his responsibility, but whenever Barius struggled financially, Antoine made up for it.

"I'll miss you, Uncle Antoine," Syndie told him. She knew that he had done his best to assist them all in anything they desired.

Barius placed the last piece of luggage in the trunk and said, "Let us go now, Antoine. We must not linger any longer."

Antoine drew his handkerchief from his back pocket and wiped tears from his eyes. *You never know what the world might bring you—the sacrifices you might have to make someday*, he thought. He knew it was for the best. He had been anticipating this great day. Despite this truth, a part of him would forever be with Barius, Julian, Syndie, and the other members of his family. He would never forget his responsibility to them. He opened the door of his seven-year-old Jeep and gave one last glance at his house. He remembered the days when he tore open sacks of cement with Margaret to help in the construction of this very house. Now, the time had come for him to leave it all behind. Leaving the house in the hands of his extended family was his only consolation.

"I am ready," Antoine said as he closed the passenger door of the car.

"We must hurry, Antoine. We don't want to be stopped by any bandits," Barius said.

As the car backed out of the driveway, Antoine could see the many faces that were filled with happiness for him yet also with slight despair.

When they pulled onto the main street, Antoine thought about his profession. This departure also meant halting his teaching career. He'd felt as if his profession was his life. He wondered how long he could last without teaching. His city had acknowledged him as a great professor. *How can I truly stop teaching?* he thought. He felt as if his social status would crumble. He had been quite productive during the years that had been bestowed to him. As a great orator, he was greatly respected, and he took pride in that. Rarely a day would pass without many acknowledging him as one of the greatest French-speaking Haitians in the country. When the president wanted to address his city, Antoine was chosen as the host. He had established his legacy on a social standpoint. He reminisced on these things because they defined who he was—one who connected with the people, was revered by the people, and was loved by the people.

He thought about losing all of his recognition.

He didn't know how America would treat him, yet he aspired to find a job that would provide him the financial means to help his wife and children and to support those abroad.

Not long afterward, it began to rain. The water poured down on the car in torrents, which reminded Antoine of the trials in life. He remembered his mom's financial struggle during his school years. He remembered the sacrifices his relatives had made in order to contribute to his education. His mom's sacrifice had made him who he was today.

As they got to Port-Au-Prince, Antoine envisioned his new life, and he could see the opportunities waiting for him abroad. He forgot the sorrowful moments that was leaving behind.

"Antoine, we're here," Barius said, his face full of anguish. "I wish you the best of luck, my brother. I sincerely hope that everything goes well for you. I hope you that prosper and remember your roots."

"Thank you, Barius. I will embrace the resources I have and make the best of them. You are now in charge. I hope that you assist the family with their requests, just as I have done," Antoine said.

"Yes, brother," Barius responded.

"Always remember—if there is anything you need, you can always count on me."

"Thank you, Antoine," Barius said.

Antoine took his luggage and entered the airport.

"May I see your ticket and passport, sir?" the receptionist asked.

"Yes, of course," Antoine responded.

He finished the checking-in process and went to the waiting room. He looked at the clock on the wall and calculated that the plane would leave in twenty minutes. *Time*, he thought, *a beautiful concept indeed. Everything comes with it, and everything leaves with it.*

There was a time when he never would have dreamed of his forthcoming departure; now, he was anticipating it.

In a short time, a voice bellowed over the ceiling speakers. "This is the final call for Flight 240 F. Departing passengers should report to gate number 3."

Antoine proceeded to the gate with a great sense of elation. He was getting closer to Margaret. He glanced at his ticket to check his seat number—12 E. He boarded the plane and placed his backpack in the overhead bin. He sat down, and within the next thirty minutes, they were twenty-thousand feet in the air.

CHAPTER 6

THE ARRIVAL

It was precisely 5:36 p.m. when Paul heard the doorbell ring and knew that his mom and dad stood behind that door. He sprang up with great alacrity. "I'm coming!" he cried. He wondered how his mom had forgotten her keys, but he really didn't care. As he opened the door, he could saw that their faces expressed utter happiness; they may have been the embodiment of it.

He was jubilant and anticipated that his parents were as well. Without acknowledging his mother's presence, he leaped into the air and embraced his father.

As Antoine walked in the house, Paul was still firmly attached to him. "How are you, Father?" Paul inquired.

"I'm doing quite well, my son," Antoine replied.

Paul had so many questions, but he knew he had to wait. As Antoine stood in front of his bedroom door, Paul noticed how slim his father's body was beneath his suit and wondered why his father was in such condition. He dismissed the thought, though; after all, his father had just arrived, and everyone was in the spirit of celebration. Paul assumed it was the stress that an under-developed country puts on an individual that had caused his father's weight loss.

As his dad and mom conversed, Paul noticed other changes about his dad. He had hoped that he would be invited to sit on his father's lap and be encouraged to speak about how life had been for him and his mom. His father never made those inquiries, however, and at that particular moment, Paul, like his father, changed. He'd always felt like he was the one asking the questions—hardly ever his dad. It was he who had hugged

23

his father with tears in his eyes; he who had hugged his father tightly. Paul dismissed the thoughts from his mind. He strongly believed that one's thoughts ruled one's life. He could not approach this situation with a pessimistic viewpoint; it must be an optimistic one. He thought of the possible rationale for the actions that had taken place. None of his ideas, however, seemed a valid explanation. He walked back to his room and lay down on his bed.

"Paul, I want you to come here," said Margaret.

Half-asleep, Paul got up from his bed and went to his mother. He knew she wanted him to spend more time with his father. As Paul sat next to Antoine, he could tell that Margaret was pleased.

"How are my cousins? Andy, Malkin, and Wawa—how are they doing, Dad?" Paul gently asked.

"They're doing quite well. They're all expecting news from me about how you are. Everyone in the family is doing quite well."

Paul then stopped speaking, which allowed his parents to continue their conversation. They discussed family affairs. His mom asked Antoine about friends with whom she had lost contact. After about thirty minutes, Paul felt exhausted. "Dad … Mom … may I be excused?"

"You may, Paul," Antoine responded.

"Thank you." Paul said, with an internal sigh of relief. Instead of going to his room, Paul entered his aunt Cheline's room. He loved Cheline dearly and always found great joy in her presence. Cheline's son is called Leny. Paul and Leny were very close.

"Leny, let's talk," Paul whispered. "My parents' conversation is quite boring. I have little interest in it. I'm very happy that my father is here. I very much expect life to better. The circumstances were just too difficult for my mom."

"We all are happy, Paul," Leny responded. "I know how you feel. Our situation is not much different. We have similar stories. I thank God that my father is here now. My mom is happier. She has a greater willingness to keep fighting in life. Paul, I am very happy with where we are right now."

"I know, Leny. I see the joy in my mom already. As long as she's happy, I believe that I will be as well. She has made many sacrifices for me and my sister, Caroline. To tell you the truth, I am perpetually concerned about her well-being."

On Sunday, everyone arose early to attend church.

"Margaret, I think I should wear this suit. What do you think of it?" Antoine inquired.

"I believe it would suit you well," she said.

Paul chose a casual shirt, sleek black pants, and nicely polished Italian shoes for his attire. He sat in the living room, trying to predict how people would perceive his dad. He was quite aware that Antoine was a well-spoken man and expressed no fear or anxiety in a public setting, and that gave Paul some consolation. He knew his father Antoine would feel ashamed nonetheless, as he feared too much attention.

"Do we have any visitors with us this morning?" asked Pastor Gregorius.

From the front two rows, Paul could see that no visitors were present, but Paul knew that there were always visitors. He looked behind him and saw the many faces that were present. In the fourth row, Paul saw his father standing up, waiting to be called on.

"Can you tell us your name, sir, and the name of the person who invited you?" asked Pastor Gregorius.

"My name is Antoine Darius, and I was invited by my beautiful wife, Margaret Darius. I am well pleased to say that I am accompanied by my beautiful daughter, Caroline, and my son, Paul."

"We're happy to have you with us, and we hope you will continue to be here. As a matter of fact, you are welcome to make your current seat permanently yours," Pastor Gregorius said.

"Thank you, thank you so much," Antoine replied with great appreciation.

Paul could tell, from where he sat, that Antoine felt welcomed.

During the service, the youth choir sang a beautiful hymn. The words "praise the Lord" resonated in the congregation. Paul felt within himself that there was a reason to praise the Lord. He hummed the melody as the youths proceeded in their song. He felt peace, a divine peace.

At the conclusion of the service, everyone got up and greeted each other individually. As Paul got in line, he noticed Ashley, a very nice young girl. She seemed as though she wanted to speak to Paul and so he approached her.

"Hey, Ashley, how are you?"

"All right, I should say. Your dad looks just like you."

"I know. I hear that a lot. Many people think we have similar characteristics too." *How could we not?* Paul thought. *He is my father.* "Bye, Ashley," Paul finally said.

For the sake of politeness and the preservation of the friendship, Paul dared not share those thoughts aloud. He had a great understanding of people's personality types. He knew that some people were offended easily, while others were not. He distanced himself from the crowd and approached the male members of the youth choir.

"Great job today, everyone. You all sang quite well. It's too bad I was unable to join you."

"It's all right, Paul. We know how hard it can be for you to make it sometimes," Jeff responded.

"Hey, Paul, I almost forgot to ask you—why is your dad so skinny? Does he have health issues? Why is he so slim?" Chris said.

"I'm not sure. I am assuming it's because of the stress Haiti put on him," Paul responded. He remembered the day his father had arrived, and he'd noticed his father's thinness as well.

"I don't think so, my friend. He might be sick," Chris said. "I suggest you have him go for a health examination."

Chris's words seemed a critical warning—even paramount—but after a brief moment of silence, they changed the topic of conversation.

"Did you watch the basketball game last night?" Jeff asked Chris.

"Of course. Who could have missed it?" Chris responded.

Paul glanced to his right and noticed the many cars waiting in line to exit the campus. He examined each as he looked for his mom's car. He could see it at the corner—his mom and dad were patiently waiting—and he ran toward them, gesturing for his mom to unlock the doors. As he entered the car, he noticed a calmness in everyone.

"We almost left you, Paul. You took a long time to leave," Caroline said.

He knew they wouldn't have left him. At the exiting turn, Paul rested his arms against the warm window and drifted asleep.

One Saturday morning, Paul noticed an electric piano and a stand that held a classical book.

"Hey, Paul, would like to learn to play the piano?" Antoine asked.

"Sure," Paul replied. He had always wanted to play the piano; he had always been fascinated by young kids who were great pianists. He gently pulled out the stool and sat.

After brief instruction, his father asked him, "What note is this?"

"I believe it's a G," Paul replied. His father frowned, and Paul knew he had given a wrong answer. "Wait, wait—I think it's an F."

"Ahh," Antoine replied, shaking his head. His patience clearly was dissipating. "How come you're not getting it?"

"I am not sure, Dad."

As the lesson continued, Paul repeatedly made similar mistakes. His dad reacted in the same manner every time. Paul felt like crying, but he knew he shouldn't. He left to take a short break and went to his mom's room. She was sitting on the edge of the bed, reading a book.

Margaret could see Paul was in distress. "Paul, what seems to be the matter, dear?"

"I don't know how to describe it," Paul said.

"Speak to me. son."

"I really think my dad is too impatient. During our piano lessons, he gets very frustrated easily. He makes me feel emotionally deprived. He's not the father I knew in Haiti. Something has drastically changed about him."

"I know, son. I have noticed it too. He's very reserved. On a personal note, he does not converse with me too much. He seems to stay on the phone with his brothers most of the time. I don't understand him either. I will pray about it and speak to him about it. This is affecting all of us."

꧁

CHAPTER 7

THE ADJUSTMENT

Within a short time, Paul's family moved into a new apartment building. With the addition of Antoine's income, they were able to afford that transition. Paul was very happy with this move, and he valued his dad more. He acknowledged the sacrifice that Antoine made every single day as his mom dropped him at the public bus station. He had gotten a job at a general merchandise store, working the night shift. Paul was not very fond of it; he believed it to put too much stress on his father's body.

"Paul, it's time to get ready. We have to drop off your dad," Margaret said.

As Paul put on his shoes, he saw his mom carefully put his dad's meal in a lunchbox. She placed each item in its appropriate position. His mom displayed a genuine love for his father.

When they arrived at the station, Paul noticed his father's willingness to work. He did not display any signs of frustration, though the work was labor-intensive. On these nights, he felt very sorry for his mom, as she was left alone with her thoughts of her husband. Paul knew that this was all part of a process. He strongly believed a time would come when their working conditions would be altered.

"Hey, Paul," Antoine said as he entered their little apartment after his shift.

"Yes, Dad?'" Paul replied with a joy that could not be masked. When his father handed Paul his lunchbox, Paul noticed the vast array of candy. As a child, candy meant a lot to him. To Paul, each candy's taste provided a unique memory. He unwrapped the Snickers bar and admired it for three seconds before taking a bite and savoring the taste. As he closed his eyes, he remembered the moments when his dad had taken him to school.

"Thank you, Dad." Paul sighed, his face beaming with gratitude and joy. "How was work?"

"It was OK. We unloaded the packages and put them in their allocated places. It was not too exhausting. Now, though, I am beginning to feel weary."

"It's all right, Dad. I think you should go to sleep."

"Hey, Dad," Caroline greeted him. She leaped in the air as she hugged her father, and they smiled at each other. Paul excused himself; he felt he should leave them. Too much affection felt bizarre to him. There were many times he felt he needed affection but didn't receive it. He categorized a hug as futile human behavior. It was his manner of coping, and it filled the emotional emptiness he felt—at least, he thought it did.

"Paul, I want you to perform at the annual church celebration," Antoine said when he arrived home one day.

"Sure, Dad."

I want the members of the congregation to know the progress you've made. This will compel them to trust me as a piano teacher, and that could make us some great revenue."

"OK, Dad," Paul responded. Paul's always wanted to obey his father. No matter how difficult the task that presented itself, Paul wanted to please God by honoring his dad.

Paul searched for a song that pertained to theme of the event and began working on it immediately. During his practice sessions, he felt touched by the song. He knew it was the perfect choice. The song spoke of the reassurance that God would be with him wherever he might be. The message was similar to that of many Christian hymns, but Paul felt a unique connection to this song.

On the day of the concert, Paul felt very anxious. When the time came for him to perform, he couldn't shake his anxiety.

"Are you ready?" Caroline asked.

"I am." He stepped on stage and boldly said, "I want to sing this to glorify God for being great to me." He got on the piano and adjusted the mike so that he could sing as he played. He sang with his soul, with his body, and with his spirit—and everyone noticed. Some of the performing artists cheered him on, and the crowd did as well.

At the conclusion of his performance, there was great applause. He directed the glory to God by pointing his finger toward the sky and then sat down.

At the conclusion of the concert, his pastor shook Paul's hand and congratulated him. Paul felt very happy. He received a thumbs-up from his father, who then ushered Paul into the car to drive home.

"Good job, son," Antoine said with an agreeable smile.

"I am very happy I did well," Paul said. *I don't know how I would have dealt with a poor performance*, he thought. Perfection meant everything for Paul. He also knew his dad tolerated no other thing.

Once at home, with his task fulfilled, Paul fell into a sweet and blissful sleep.

CHAPTER 8

DISHEARTENING NEWS

At one o'clock in the morning, Paul heard his bedroom doorknob turning and heard his mom enter. She tapped him on the shoulder, and he asked her why she was there.

"I had to take your dad to the emergency room."

"Why?" Paul asked, now consumed with worry.

"He told me he felt a pain in his lower abdomen and demanded that I take him to the hospital."

Paul saw sadness in his mother's eyes, and he could tell that she had been weeping; it was then that he knew something was terribly wrong.

"The doctors told me that based on the analysis of what they have seen, they think he might have cancer," Margaret whispered.

Paul suddenly felt drained of all strength. He saw tears welling up in his mother's eyes, although she seemed to not want him to see her weep. He picked up his courage and tried to console her, for he knew nothing was impossible for God to accomplish.

Still, although his soul had a strong reassurance, his body was weak, and he spent the whole night weeping.

The next day, he went to visit his dad in the hospital. Antoine had a smile on his face, which gave Paul comfort. Paul shook his dad's hands firmly, praying his dad had the courage to do the same. Antoine responded accordingly, and Paul sat by his side.

When the nurse entered, Paul asked for a better explanation of what was wrong with his dad, but she was under the code of HIPAA and could not reply.

Paul felt a rush of sadness, but tried to repel it with prayer. *Why is such calamity befalling us?* Paul asked God. He waited, hoping God would immediately respond. With no reply, he sat down until his mom took him home.

Caroline was only six, and he started to wonder what effect his dad's death would have on her. *Could she be raised without a dad at such a young age?* he wondered. His sister had only known her dad for three years. She had only stayed in Haiti for three months before she immigrated to the United States. He tried to stop himself from thinking negative thoughts and fought to conjure positive ones, but he found himself thinking about his situation more and more. He had many dreams and wanted his father to be part of them. He had always dreamed of his dad being at his graduations and even his wedding. He had hoped his father would be present for anything that he planned to achieve. He wanted his father's counsel; he wanted to be led by his father's example. Somewhere within Paul, he wanted to be a miniature Antoine. He had a great respect for who his dad was, what he had accomplished, and how hard he'd worked on the things that he aspired to do.

How will his absence affect my upbringing? he thought.

Questions entered his mind at one hundred miles per hour, and nothing he tried could stop them.

While waiting for the diagnosis of his dad's condition, Paul felt complete sorrow. It wasn't until three weeks later that the results finally came.

Margaret had made an appointment with Antoine's specialist soon after his hospitalization. She did not want to believe that Antoine had a serious condition. Paul waited eagerly to hear the news. His fingers were tightly crossed, his heart pounded in his chest, and his mind was filled with thoughts.

After many hours of waiting, his mom finally came home, and Paul could tell that something was terribly wrong. He noticed the sadness on his mom's face and her wavering gait as she entered the apartment.

"What did the specialist say?" he asked.

"He told me your dad has liver cancer," she replied. "He said that due to the size of the cancer, surgery could be fatal, and that at this point, chemotherapy would be ineffective. Your dad was prescribed some medications to reduce the size of the malignant tumor so that chemotherapy could be initiated."

At that moment, Paul's legs gave up the strength they'd had; his mind gave up its stability; and his soul, its serenity. He knew he had to leave the room; the circumstances called for it. He couldn't let his mom see him in such a state of anguish. He rushed to his mom's room to hide his behavior.

He wept and wept until there were no more tears left.

Soon afterward, Paul became angry—angry that he was the only child he knew who was going through such a trial. "Why does it have to be me?" he asked repeatedly.

His attitude changed as well; it became downright acerbic. When asked if he needed help, he would sharply reply, "I'm fine."

"Are you sure?" the person would ask, but Paul always responded with a glare that sent a clear message: *Leave me alone.*

He despised the sympathy that others expressed. He did not like that other people felt sorry for him, especially when it was for a circumstance over which he was powerless. He began to hate some of the church members because of their sympathetic approach. He was angry, and as a young boy, he was not sure how to react. *Sympathy is for those who fail to fulfill their responsibilities*, he thought. *Could there be another rational reason?* He had done everything in his power to honor his mom and dad; this was not his fault. Paul felt a heavy burden on his shoulders.

≈

CHAPTER 9

WHEN A CHILD PRAYS

At 5:00 a.m., Paul was awakened by the alarm on his phone. It was time for him to get ready for school. He took his blue scrubs from his wardrobe and laid them on a flat surface to iron them. As he ironed, he thought of the omniscience of God. He was the only being who gave Paul a stability of mind.

Paul finished with his preparation and left the house. On his way to the bus stop, he became conscious of the darkness that enveloped him. He had never been so aware of his surroundings. He felt safe because of his faith in God as he walked to his designated bus stop. From a distance, he noticed Lydian listening to music through a pair of white headphones. Paul knew that she was fond of him, but she couldn't muster the courage and maturity to tell him. Paul chuckled at the thought. It was not a humorous chuckle, as sorrow was the theme of his life at that particular moment. Paul waved at her; she waved back and stared at him for some time; then she resumed her solitude. She had always been introverted around him, but Paul knew that was not her natural state.

Should I tell her what I am going through? Paul thought. *What would she think about it? Would she tell others if I don't want them to know?* The stakes were too high; he could not risk this story being told among his peers. He could not afford them feeling sympathy for him as well. He already imagined all of the people saying, "I am so sorry."

The bus arrived, and Paul boarded after Lydian. He found a seat near the back of the bus near the window. He took his phone from his backpack and opened his music application. Looking through his song lists, he found with the words, "Why do you cry?" It was a question he had asked himself for so many weeks. Every time he witnessed his father's deterioration, he would cry. He knew God was omniscient, yet he still cried—although it hardly ever was noticeable. This situation was different. Life was changing at an alarming pace. All of the hope that his dad had brought when he came to America was slowly fading away.

The bus turned onto the high school campus and stopped to let the students off. Paul rushed to the soccer field, which was obscured by the early morning darkness. He stood near a portable that completely shielded him from any view. He removed his backpack and began to pray.

"Lord, God almighty, who created the heavens, the earth, and everything therein, I praise you for who you are. I extol your name because you created me and not me alone. Surely, I am one of your people and the sheep of thy pasture. I pray that you forgive my sins and my iniquities. I pray that you will cleanse me from my carnal state of being. It is you I love; it is you I desire. Lord, I pray that you will stabilize me emotionally so that I can endure my struggles. God, my father is very ill. I believe that you can touch him and heal him. Lord, please have mercy upon him. I implore you, please touch him. In Jesus Christ's divine and wondrous name, I pray. Amen."

At the conclusion of his prayer, Paul felt compelled to sing a hymn. "Precious Lord," he sang, "take my hand." Oh, how he sought to be led. He earnestly desired to be led by a being who knew the way—the way to happiness, the way to the tranquility that would not waver. He was shaking during this part of his worship. He invoked God with every ounce of his being. God was Paul's only hope.

Looking to his left, he saw the students walking to their first-period classes. He figured the bell had rung, but he hadn't heard it. He took his backpack and jogged to his English 1 honors class. He had always been fond of English. Mr. Bardin, his current English teacher, was perhaps the best instructor he'd had.

"Good morning, Paul," Mr. Bardin said with a welcoming smile.

"Hello, Mr. Bardin. How are you?"

"I am doing swell, thank you," replied Mr. Bardin with an appreciative nod.

Paul sat down and looked at the chalkboard, which had the word *jargon* written on it. He wrote it down in his notebook and defined it as unintelligible speech. Mr. Bardin always gave them a word each day to write.

"Can anyone tell me why one would use a semicolon in formal writing?" Mr. Bardin asked.

Paul raised his hand eagerly. *Pick me*, he thought.

"Paul, can you please tell us?"

"Yes, it is used to separate two independent clauses that are relevant to each other."

"Correct," Mr. Bardin responded. "We also use the semicolon to …"

Paul jotted down the information he considered essential and listened attentively.

When the class discussion began, Paul remarked that it involved the meaning of life. As the teacher made them look over many literary texts, Paul acknowledged that the authors' philosophies lacked insight.

"What do you guys believe is the meaning of life?" Mr. Bardin asked the class.

"It has to do with whatever makes you happy," Leonard responded.

Paul thought Leonard's answer implied self-gratification. Many had that conviction, and Paul could not blame them. It took a lot for one to achieve self-denial.

"No, it has to do with your required duty in society," Jasmine said.

"What is your definition, Paul?" Mr. Bardin inquired.

Paul thought for a moment. He did not know how to answer the question. Thankfully, the bell rang, and everyone began to gather their things. Paul shook his head to indicate that he did not know. At last, he responded, "All is vanity. The only thing that really matters is how someone lives for Jesus Christ." He'd told the class, but he'd whispered that to himself.

As he anticipated second period, Paul's heart began to race. He noticed Andy, an athletic boy who many students revered.

"Hey, Andy!"

Andy raised his finger to show he acknowledged Paul's greeting. Andy was wearing his headphones as they walked to class. Paul had known him for some time, but Andy never initiated conversations. He always waited to be questioned. To Paul, he was a king. Andy was not much of a talker, except to those who shared similar interests. Paul fancied sports, but he didn't think of it as being his career. Andy, however, played sports because he believed it was a great way of becoming successful.

"Bruce, Karen, Andy, Paul!" called Coach Justin.

"Here," they each responded. Five minutes into the class, the teacher handed them their tests. Within twenty minutes, Paul had answered each question and turned in the test. When everyone had finished, they were allowed to choose an activity for the remainder of the class. Paul chose basketball and joined Andy on the courts.

"Paul, would you like to play ball?" Andy asked.

Paul complied. The game was quite aggressive, and Andy dominated throughout it. Paul had expected that; after all, sports meant a lot to Andy, and he worked very hard at it.

After the game, Zach and Joseph asked if they could join in another game. Paul was confident of Andy's ability to score, so he chose Andy as his teammate.

After a couple of passes between each other and failed scoring attempts, Andy bellowed, "Why are you missing those easy shots? What don't you understand about scoring a layup?"

There were two things that Paul had always resented: conversations that involved yelling and the use of obscene language. He was confronted with a dilemma; he could continue playing with Andy to preserve their friendship, or he could leave the game to show his resentment. He chose the latter; he believed he deserved to be respected.

"You don't want to play anymore?" Andy inquired.

"No, I'm all right."

Paul found a section of the bleachers where many of his peers were sitting. He thought of Andy's action and the lack of wisdom involved. In order to be respectful at all times, one had to be humble. Even in times of anger, humility would abate it and cause you to treat others respectfully.

With the final bell for the day, Paul raced to his bus. As he boarded, he heard a loud commotion and the rude conversations the students were having.

"Hey, Pastor," Richard teased Paul.

The students burst into laughter. Paul figured the word was appropriate for him, due to the many ways he failed to conform to their standards. There were many obscenities uttered on the bus, which Paul found deplorable. He felt disconnected to God as he listened to the students' conversations. Their topics were deplorable too, and their laughter was overly exuberant. They displayed an absence of shame in their actions.

This was a daily occurrence for Paul, and the only way he could cope with it was by attempting to sleep. Whenever he would drift into unconsciousness, however, shrieking laughter or a deafening yell would bring him back to reality. After about two hours, the bus reached Paul's stop, and he departed.

Lydian went her way, and he went his. The sun felt unbearable to Paul. He passed the plaza near his home and jogged as he got closer. He wanted to see his father, who was back home now. He wanted to assess his father's condition.

When he opened the door, he noticed his father sitting on the couch, listening to a Haitian radio station. Paul never understood why his father did that. He failed to understand why someone living in America would be concerned about the news in Haiti.

"How are you, Dad?" Paul asked as he shook Antoine's hand.

"I'm doing good, my son. This Saturday, we have a doctor's appointment in Miami, and we would like you to join us."

Paul knew it was not optional; his dad just wanted Paul to be aware of their upcoming meeting. Paul saw it as an opportunity to better understand his father's condition. He wanted to know if there was still hope.

CHAPTER 10

DR. FUN

That Saturday, Paul sensed his mom's anxiety. As he approached his parents' bedroom, he overheard his dad ask, "Do you think there is still a chance?"

"It will be all right, Antoine. I believe anything is possible," Margaret replied.

After they finished their conversation, Paul entered the room and noticed many documents on the bed. He saw the doctor's referral and his dad's insurance card. He also noticed that his father had reached a breaking point. With so much left to accomplish, death was not the outcome to which his father aspired. *No one wants to die from stage IV liver cancer*, Paul thought. He could tell that his dad's patience had diminished. If Antoine misplaced anything, he would get angry at himself. It was as if his condition was the result of inaction.

Antoine hadn't noticed any symptoms of liver cancer in Haiti, but he was unsure of its etiology. He had an unwillingness to perish, so he had an internal struggle. Now, Antoine finished arranging everything in his briefcase and gestured to his wife.

"Let's go, Paul," Margaret said.

Once they were in the car, Margaret said, "Paul, can you please put the address in the GPS for me?"

"Yes, Mom," Paul obediently answered.

They all fastened their seatbelts, and Margaret handed Paul the phone to set the GPS. He realized that the doctor they would see worked at a university. They were going there to get a second opinion.

As a reasonable individual, Antoine insisted on getting a second perspective on his condition. Margaret and Antoine were not satisfied with Dr. Andrew's opinion on the matter. He had referred them to Dr. Fun because he was one of the most experienced doctors in the field of oncology.

Regarding treatments, Antoine wanted to know the best one for him or that would give him the best chance of survival. He did not just want palliative care. He refused to believe that his time had come, and comfort care was not his desire. He was willing go through whatever treatment was necessary. Even if it had to be radical, that did not concern him; he had to be treated.

When they arrived at the university, they were politely directed to the appropriate department. The front of the building was a pleasant cream color. Many doctors were moving from one department to another. *They must be medical students in residency*, Paul thought. *They all have their lab coats on.*

"Antoine," said a woman who received them in reception room. "Dr. Fun is ready to see you now." She opened the door to a hallway with many more doors. They were then seated in a room, and within two minutes, an elderly Asian doctor entered the room.

"Good morning. I am Dr. Fun," he said softly.

They all replied "Good morning" in unison.

How could Dr. Andrew refer us a to an oncology doctor named Dr. Fun? Paul thought.

"I see here, Antoine, that you desire a second opinion of your condition and that you wish to know the available treatments. Is that correct?"

"Yes," Antoine responded.

Dr. Fun gestured to Paul. "Would you like to have him interpret for you?"

"Yes," Antoine responded.

"Your father has stage IV cancer, and it only seems to be spreading. I strongly recommend radiation to help reduce the size of the tumor. Then we will use chemotherapy to treat the malignancy."

Paul turned to his father and translated the information Dr. Fun had given.

"Ask him about other treatments," Antoine said.

"Apart from the radiation and the chemotherapy, what other treatments are available?" Paul asked Dr. Fun.

"I am afraid to tell you that the other possible option is the medication he has been taking. I have here in his report that Antoine is not responding well to it. I see that he's been vomiting after taking it."

"Yes, that is true. It also makes him bedridden," Paul said. He leaned toward his father to facilitate the communication and told him what Dr. Fun had said.

Dr. Fun then presented Antoine with a package that included an agreement to proceed with the radiation therapy. With the state he was in, Antoine felt he had no choice.

Paul could see the desperation on his dad's face.

"Is this guaranteed to work?" he asked Paul.

Paul looked at Dr. Fun with a very serious expression and repeated his dad's question.

"I'm afraid that the other treatment we're offering is still under development," Dr. Fun said. "Some patients have tried it, and it has improved their health, but others have had negative responses. We do not know how your body will respond to it; therefore, we cannot give you any guarantees. It is completely up to you."

Paul saw his mother gently bow her head. He could see the grief she felt. Paul was shaken too. His dad had hoped that Dr. Fun's words would be full of reassurance. Paul had hoped for it too. Antoine's condition was so critical that Paul felt inclined toward hope—that was the only thing he could do. His dad had reached a point where nothing was certain.

Dr. Fun gave them some time to regain their composure. He himself appeared sad too, as well as confounded. He knew they sought an answer, but he had none to give. Paul knew that when a doctor, in whom most had utter faith, displayed any signs of helplessness, then most hope was lost.

"I have the CAT scan results here," Dr. Fun finally said.

Paul stood up so that he could look at the images more clearly. One-fourth of the liver had malignant cells. It was very apparent.

"The truth is, only 10 percent of the liver is functioning," Dr. Fun explained.

"At what rate is the liver losing its function?" Paul asked.

"We do not know. That's a smart question," Dr. Fun replied. He then reviewed the terms and conditions with the family. Each of the conditions was quite simple. It involved the basic consent requests: Do you want to proceed with this treatment? Do you understand the risks involved?

Paul could tell that Margaret felt it was the only option.

Antoine, too, felt as if he had no other choice, and he signed the consent to receive the radiation.

"Do you have any other questions?" Dr. Fun asked.

Paul glanced at his father and noticed him shaking his head in a manner that showed he did not have any questions.

Dr. Fun understood the nonverbal communication and said, "Remember that you have an appointment in four months so we can inform you of the status of your condition and any improvements."

At the end of the visit, a very nice young nurse helped them find their way out. They were ushered to the main stairway, which was made of marble. If Paul had been at the university for something less serious, he would have raced down the stairs to find his way out, but he was here because his father was critically sick. This was not the time for him to behave like a child.

He noticed the manner in which he walked and slowed down a little bit to make sure he was not walking too fast. He walked near his dad, so that if Antoine lost his balance, Paul could support him. During their walk, Paul could tell that his dad's physique had diminished drastically. Even though Paul knew his dad had stage IV liver cancer, and he had seen pictures of diseased livers, he had not conceptualized the degree of his father's condition. Paul remembered the image he had seen at the office, and he shivered at the sight in his head. The liver lobes were almost completely enveloped in cancerous cells.

When they finally reached the car and got in, everyone stayed silent for some time. There was not much Paul could do. Prayer, for him, was his only hope. He knew that even if the treatment proved effective, his father would eventually die.

Perhaps it could give him a couple of years more, yet everyone would know that was it. Antoine was going to die; there was no other hope. *Wait*, Paul thought, *maybe there is.* It would take a miracle indeed for Antoine to regain his healthy state. God would have to directly intervene. *One reaches a state in life that if God does not intervene, one will undoubtedly perish.* As Paul leaned on the window, he thought of the reality of the matter.

He understood that men do not die when they're struck by an incurable malignancy; rather, they die when the believe nothing is possible. It is when they have this belief that they cease to look for answers, but Paul knew that there always is hope in God. Even though that contradicted the reasoning of men, Paul believed it was an absolute truth. He took consolation in this truth. After all, the very scriptures that he had read told him that "anything is possible if someone believes."

He also knew that the contrary was true. Nothing is possible for those who do not believe. Antoine was a man of logic—if he could perceive, then he could not believe. The problem could not be approached on a carnal standpoint; it had to be a spiritual one. Paul struggled to believe that his dad had a chance—not because the cancer was spreading but because his dad harbored a state of unbelief. Paul detected it when Dr. Fun had said there were no other options. The seed grew even more when Dr. Fun said that the treatment was not guaranteed to solve the condition. Paul saw the despair on his dad's face and noticed the sudden drop of his shoulders, the slight shift of his foot. Paul knew that the news had overtaken Antoine. Instead of being encouraged, he felt discouraged. Paul could see it all. He'd thought his dad's faith was unshakable, but now he wondered whether it was ever there.

When they arrived in their neighborhood, Paul saw the leaves swaying and felt the sweet coolness of the wind as the sun set. As they approached their apartment, Paul saw a squirrel frantically burying a nut, but when it noticed them, it aborted its mission and ran up a tree. Paul also noticed a duck with her ducklings. They all stayed close to their mom, likely feeling more protected when they were close to their mom. *What humanistic behavior*, Paul thought.

His mother opened the white front door to their home. Paul always felt happy when he reached home. This was where he resided; this was his sanctuary. As he took a step past his mom, he noticed something different about her. She had streaks of tears across her cheeks that she forgotten to wipe away.

Paul decided to play the piano and chose Chopin's Prelude op. 28, no.20. He had to play this classical piece. It was critical that he express his grief though song. Although he felt compelled to cry, he knew it would only mitigate his grief. Playing music gave him clearer thoughts; it allowed his mind to drift away from reality and temporarily placed him in a state of illusion. The music was his form of escape. Whatever his body could not handle, he allowed it to freely flow through his music. The only sad reality was that people who were listening would begin to feel what he had been feeling.

He noticed his mother reading her Bible on the patio. She was reading her psalms out loud as she sought the Lord for help. He could hear the anguish in her voice. She spoke in a tone that displayed her desperation in the highest degree. She had taken it upon herself to seek the Lord for her husband's healing. It was a unique sight; it taught Paul to seek God when things were not going well. He went to his parents' room, as he wondered what his father was doing. He found him lying in bed, watching a soccer match.

Paul was dumbfounded. *How can he possibly be watching a match after learning such heartbreaking news?* He pretended that he was getting something and quickly departed. His mom, who was not sick, displayed more concern for Antoine's condition than Antoine himself. *That's absurd*, Paul thought.

Unable to hide his anger, he decided to confront his father. He took to some time to think of a respectful approach and then reentered the room. "Dad, I suggest you read the Bible. The doctor's news seemed very serious."

"Don't worry, son. Everything will be just fine." He continued watching television as if his son's words meant nothing to him.

At that moment, once more, Paul felt unappreciated. He wondered whether his dad would ever take him—or anyone in his family—seriously. Whenever his mom gave Antoine advice, he seemed to always reject it or find a reason to object. He confided only in his brothers and sisters. He cherished their words; he valued them and tried his best to take them into profound consideration.

CHAPTER 11

THE VISITATION

One starry evening, Paul heard a knock on the door.

Antoine's condition had not reached a debilitating point, so he withdrew the sheet that covered him and went to greet his sister Julian. As he beheld her, he was happy. This was the sister who had been like a mother when he was growing up. He felt very connected to her, despite being away from her for the past two years. They hugged for some time before they spoke.

"How's everyone in Haiti," Antoine inquired.

"They're doing quite well. The children are going to school, and everyone is fairly happy."

"I am very happy to hear that," he said. "When I got the news that you had gotten a visa to visit this country, I was very happy. It has been too long since I've seen you. The health crisis has been one of the hardest things of my life. The good news is that the side effects I'd felt from my medications have almost seemed to vanish."

As he continued to speak, he began to feel fatigued. His body was wearing out. "Let's speak in my room, Julian."

"Oh, OK," she said in a sympathetic voice. She followed Antoine into his room and said, "Hello, Margaret."

"How are you, Julian? How are the children?" Margaret asked.

"They're doing quite well," she responded.

Margaret got up to fix the appropriate meals for the visit. His wife loved to welcome her guests, particularly his extended family members.

"How are you feeling, Antoine," Julian inquired after Margaret left.

"I am hanging in there, sister. The medications are quite radical. They are very hard to take due to the side effects. I had been vomiting three times a day until recently. As I speak to you, I can feel a sharp pain in my lower abdomen."

"You'll get better."

"I hope so. I can't imagine leaving my son and daughter behind. There is so much that they have yet to learn. I really wish I could do more for them."

"You have done a lot, Antoine. You know who you are. You know what you have accomplished. Continue to take pride in that. Even if things were to go wrong, you will never be forgotten. To tell you the truth, I do not believe that anything will go wrong."

"You are right, Julian. I am hopeful, but if anything happens, make sure I am buried in Haiti. I cannot imagine the cost and the burden it would be on Margaret if it were to happen here. I have told this to Mark, but if he decides not to comply, persuade him."

Margaret entered the room and said, "Everything is ready, Julian. You may come to the table any time you choose."

"I am coming, Margaret," Julian responded. "You know, Margaret, I believe that my family is my brothers—not my children or anyone else. The reality is that a child may leave you, a husband may leave, but it is much harder for a sister or a brother to leave his kin"

"Interesting," Margaret replied.

Antoine was happy to know that Julian perceived him in such a way. He knew that Margaret could have taken the words in the wrong way, but he did not have the will to think much of it. His life was fading from his sight. He wanted to cherish every moment that he had left.

He gathered his strength and walked to the table. As everyone ate, Antoine thought of how his friends perceived him. He felt as if he was at life's mercy—the worst feeling he ever experienced.

"Antoine, I have your food here," Margaret said. "It is specifically designed for you."

He examined it closely and could see that it was a green mixture of organic vegetables and a drink that contained many herbs. He felt irritated. He was appalled that he could not consume every food that he desired. He knew it was necessary, yet he was unhappy. "Margaret, why do I have to eat this?" he asked. He could not resist the question. He was not pleased with what he was being fed.

As Margaret heard his words, a teardrop fell from her eye and onto the table, and Antoine was touched by it. He did not want to hurt the woman he had loved for so many years. She was the one who had made many difficult sacrifices so that he could endure his sufferings.

"I'm trying to help you, Antoine," Margaret said. "I want you to get better.

She was right, he realized. It was her wish for him to recover, but greater still, he *had* to recover. It was necessary. He thought once more of society's perception of him. He imagined fellow church members speaking of his hardship. That felt more horrible than the pain his body was experiencing.

He finished his dinner and withdrew to the patio. He opened the radio app on his phone to listen to his country's news. This was his way of escaping reality. Whenever he heard of the sorrows of others, he could forget his own.

"This is Radio Metropol. We have the data on product prices. We now know that the prices of consumer products have skyrocketed. Furniture commodities have increased by 12 percent, the price of gas by 8 percent, and food prices have increased by 2 percent," the announcer said.

Antoine felt dismayed. *Whenever there is a bad government administration, the people will suffer,* he thought.

He was not allowed to drive because Margaret feared that something might go wrong when he was behind the wheel. He began to feel limited— the one feeling he had dreaded for his entire life.

"Where are you going, Antoine?" Julian asked.

"Upstairs. I have a friend in a third-floor apartment. I want to spend some time with him." He only wanted to watch a soccer game with his friend, but he had to give him a stronger reason.

"I'm here now, Antoine," Julian said. "You may speak to me."

"I know," he responded as he walked out and then closed the door.

He made his way to the elevator and thought of the soccer game. He loved his national team, yet they were too inexperienced to go too far. He knew that was the truth. He finally made his way to door 219. He knocked and waited for Junior to open.

"Hey, Antoine."

"How have been doing?" Antoine asked.

"All right," Junior responded.

With that, Antoine entered the apartment, and they spoke of matters that interested them.

"What do you think of the upcoming election?" Junior asked Antoine.

"I believe that it will be unique. Never has it been in Haiti's history that a president served longer than his designated term."

Antoine answered his friend's questions with intellectual comments. He believed his responses were coherent and rational. For Antoine, this was a critical factor in showing that he was a highly educated man.

CHAPTER 12

THE DISAPPROVAL

Margaret was very surprised by Julian's visit. She had been told that she was coming, but she had not known the exact date. She was not very fond of Julian; she saw her as conspicuously mischievous.

Margaret remembered the many times that Julian had spoken untruthful things about her. She knew that Julian admired Antoine's wealth and could not bear that Margaret had helped him amass his fortune. Margaret had heard that Julian had become a Christian, but she was not sure about that. She had not been given an opportunity to confirm it. She had learned from experience that it was one's conduct that reflected Jesus Christ in a person.

"Mom, I don't like how Aunt Julian has been treating me," Caroline said. "She reprimands me for everything I say. She exaggerates it. She accuses me continually."

"It's all right, sweetheart," Margaret said, wanting to be supportive. "She will only be staying for a couple of days, although maybe longer, if necessary. Just try to avoid her."

Caroline was a very talkative girl who loved to express her emotions. Whenever she felt emotionally distressed, she would write letters explaining how she felt. Paul was like that too, but he never showed his writing to anyone. Caroline would approach Margaret and share the moment in a story.

Margaret took her daughter's remarks seriously, but in this particular situation, she was not sure how to approach Julian. She wanted to avoid that woman herself. Julian loved to create dissention. Margaret wondered what Julian's true purpose was. She knew that concern for Antoine's condition was not Julian's only objective; spiritual insight told her that.

One night, as Margaret slept on some sheets that she had laid on the floor, she slowly awoke and noticed Julian staring at her with a look of resentment. Julian sat at a table with a glass of pomegranate juice and stared at Margaret incessantly.

Margaret felt insecure as she inspected Julian's gaze. Julian couldn't see that Margaret was awake, as her eyelids were hidden by the light, so Julian continued to stare. Margaret then had confirmation that her eyes were hidden when Julian spoke in an unbelievable whisper.

"You think that he's going to die, and you will live. Well, we will see about that. As soon as he dies, you die."

Margaret was shocked. She did not want to believe the words that came from Julian's mouth. She had known that Julian despised her but not to that extent. She closed her eyes and tried to prevent any unwanted events. She did not want Julian to know that she knew of her heart's wishes. At least, Margaret thought it was only a wish. Still, she felt as if it was something much more, something more profound.

She felt as if Julian uttered those words with conviction; It was not just a wish but something certain that she knew would happen and was anticipating. Margaret felt that the words were certain.

She had to be cautious. She had to be careful of any plot that Julian might conceive.

CHAPTER 13

TRAITOR IN THE HOME

Paul had known his aunt but didn't understand her. He knew she was admired by some and despised by many.

One day when Paul came home from school, he heard a voice that was familiar to him. It was the voice of a woman who had not spoken to him for nine years; it was his aunt. Fearing that he would disrupt the conversation, he quietly opened the door and entered the apartment. She was about five feet in height, commonly large in width, with a countenance that appeared emotionless. She was smiling. No, she was laughing. Unsure whether it was genuine, Paul inspected her for some time longer. Unsurprisingly, Paul noticed her facial expressions changed too rapidly and her slight body movements indicated profound tension. Perhaps she did not want to be part of the conversation but felt it was necessary.

I hate conformists, Paul thought. *They lack originality*. With a swift motion, he kicked off his shoes. Unable to avoid her, he walked toward Julian in a straightforward manner to greet her. It was part of his culture for young people to greet female adults with a kiss on the cheek. He had to please his mom and dad, as they sat there and entertained her.

"How are you doing, Aunt Julian?" Paul asked as he lowered his cheeks to the same height as hers. He leaned forward in a motion that would provide the slightest touch. For him, it was necessary that the touch was slight and quick. He did not feel comfortable around Aunt Julian.

"How are you, Paul?" she inquired, trying, with great effort, to display the greatest sincerity. She was not successful in her effort. The smile paused halfway, and her breath emitted an air of dissent.

It's cold, Paul thought. *Yes, it's frigid. It reflects the condition of her soul.* He pulled away, constraining his muscles to move slowly—at a speed that was half of his desire—and then proceeded to his tasks.

There was something about her that made him feel extremely uncomfortable. Whenever he moved around in their apartment, she checked on whether he was watching her, which made her seem suspicious. On other occasions, she acted in a manner that was outside her authority.

"Paul, I need your phone," she said.

"Give me some time, Aunt. It is important that I master this piece of music," he responded in a pleading manner, assuming that she would understand. For some time, there was silence, and Paul thought she had consented. He proceeded with his music, using his phone as his metronome.

Then, he felt steps approaching him from behind. The stool under him slightly shook, a result of the power of the steps. Before he could to turn around, a small hand reached across his shoulder and grabbed the phone. Paul felt his heart race, and he felt threatened. His personal space had been invaded. He turned around to see who had committed such act. Three feet away from him stood Julian, with one hand clutching his phone—his property—and the other hand on her hip. She had the expression of someone who had gone mad, someone who was avenging, and perhaps someone who felt justified.

Paul hoped that she would apologize and confess that her behavior was inappropriate, that it was a result of her inability to control her emotions. He hoped that she would say something such as, "Your refusal to give me the phone when I expected it caused me to act immaturely."

Her pride, however, was too great for such acts. Her look indicated it, her posture confirmed it, and her piercing eyes dared Paul to do something about it.

He sighed, knowing that there was no way he could confront his aunt. He did not have the right to be displeased; that was part of his culture. Julian was his superior, and an inferior does not oppose superiors. As Paul thought about this implied custom in his culture, he thought of how unfair it was. It promoted injustice to those unable to help themselves.

Paul shook his head, stood from his piano, and walked away. He could not afford to think of his aunt's actions. He felt his anger rising; he would always feel that way in circumstance such as those. In the cold breeze of the passing air, he inhaled a deep breath to calm his anger.

⌒

A BROKEN HEART

It was rainy that day. The water flowed, but there was a tranquility that could not have come from any other weather condition. Paul entered his home hurriedly and rushed to his closet in search of dry clothes that would warm him. In the corner of his wardrobe, he noticed his favorite light-blue long-sleeved shirt. It was warm but also gave him self-confidence. Whenever he wore that blue shirt, he felt very different. It gave him of a feeling of invincibility. He felt quite secure and protected. He knew it was an illusion—God was his true confidence—but he loved that shirt.

"Dad, may I speak to you," Paul asked. He needed to talk to someone. His mother wasn't home, and he just wanted someone to speak to.

"About what?" Antoine asked.

"I don't know, Dad. I just want to talk, I guess."

"If you don't have anything specific to say, why do you want to speak to someone?"

Paul had hoped his father would understand, but now he felt as if his dad had forgotten what it was like to be human. *I am a social being, and he's my father. I should be able to have a normal conversation with him*, he thought.

Paul felt that died that evening. His father's reasoning had killed him.

All Paul could do was resolve to write a letter. He needed to write one to stop his thoughts. He loved his dad, yet his dad did not love him. *Wait—perhaps he did, but his actions did not show it.*

Paul turned away ... shattered ... broken ... humiliated. He nodded as he turned, nodded to signify that his father was right. He was just a boy. He could not object; he could not question; he could only agree and comply. This was his responsibility. He tried to keep his facial expression emotionless, but he knew he only had ten seconds. He opened the white doors and made his way to his computer desk. He pulled out a sheet of lined paper and took the cap off his blue pen. He stared at it, attempting to collect his thoughts in an acceptable manner. He began to write what he did not have the courage to say in his father's presence.

> *Dear Dad,*
>
> *I wish that you would speak to me in a friendly way.*
> *I wish that you smiled at me when I'm depressed. I wish that ... you would not give me harsh answers that turn me away.*
> *I wish that you would recognize me as your son and never ask me to leave you alone.*
> *I wish that you that treated me as your own and made me feel at home.*
> *You know that I don't treat you in disrespectful ways, so please give me your love, and I will be OK.*
>
> *Sincerely,*
> *Paul*

Tears flowed from his eyes. He understood what it was like to feel unloved and rejected. *Yes, rejection is the word.* Unless a matter was of great interest to Antoine, he would not have a lengthy conversation with Paul. Antoine did not know how to handle jokes, nor could he see the yearnings that his child had. *Perhaps this is a direct result of his illness*, Paul thought. As Antoine's condition got worse, he became more introverted and seemed almost robotic.

Paul remembered another time when he'd tried to start a conversation.

"Dad, I found a bag full of money in my school's trash can."

"You did?" Antoine inquired, with eyes that sparkled with interest.

"Yes, as I went to dispose of my trash, I noticed the bag, and after careful inspection, I noticed that money was in it."

"Margaret!" Antoine called. "Did you hear what Paul just said?"

Before the conversation could go any farther, Paul felt compelled to tell the truth. "I'm just kidding, Dad. I didn't actually find a bag with money in it."

"Paul, you can't joke with me like that. I thought you were serious. Don't ever do that to me again," he commanded.

Paul felt ashamed. He had not expected such harsh responses. He only had wanted to speak of a matter that interested him. He wondered whether his father would have responded similarly eight months earlier.

He left the room and attempted to get involved in an activity that would help him forget the experience.

"Paul, you see that your father's character is changing. Try to avoid him. Maybe he will change as he gets better," Margaret said as she entered the living room.

"It will never get better, Mom. My dad will always be who he is. He cares about his own interests. You know that, Mom. You know that."

"I know, son, but trust that God will change him."

◈

CHAPTER 15

RATIONAL POINT OF VIEW

Antoine could feel his condition getting worse by the day. The treatment that Dr. Fun had suggested for him was not effective. On the day of his radiation infusion, it was found that the cancer had metastasized to a degree that would not warrant proceeding with the treatment.

He entered that university's surgery room and saw the doctors waiting for him. There were many student doctors waiting to dissect him to try to remove some of his liver. Later, he was conscious of the doctors staring at him as his procedure ended.

He had not felt any pain, but he did feel the incisions. He'd felt himself being marked for a procedure that did not give him any guarantees. He was a man of reason; he always had lived with an if/then point of view. Now, in this nicely lit room, he was put in the hands of men. He believed in men, as long as they were rational, as long as long as their theories were tangible and observable and were acknowledged by his perceptions. He did not encourage foolishness, nor could he bring himself to accept and submit to spiritual thinking, yet he was aware that this affected him every day. He always saw the spiritual aspect of humankind in a theoretical perspective. He did not understand that they were expedient. His great struggle was submitting to acts that he could not rationally explain.

As he lay on the table, he thought of his God, the very being who formed the universe. *Wait ...* he thought.

He had not manifested the concept of faith. He had to pray, not to his God but rather to his wife's God. He prayed that the God of his wife would enable him to go through a speedy surgery, and he prayed that all of the possible mistakes would not happen. As a rational man, he knew that trial and error was a possibility, but he could not afford it in such situation. No, he could not, but he was in the hands of men.

After eight hours, he was conscious in recovery and was told he could go home. He was very surprised that such a surgery did not require a long hospitalization. He wondered about the time he would need to recover. He hoped that his convalescence period would be short.

"Do you have a ride coming for you?" one of the doctors inquired.

"Yes," he replied, "my brother Mark is coming in twenty-five minutes." He looked at the clock, and sure enough, it was five thirty-five. His brother had agreed to come at six.

He felt fine for a while and thought he was OK. Then, around 5:50 p.m., he felt a sharp pain in the lower left quadrant of his abdomen. It was abrupt, yet noticeable, and sharp enough for it to stay in his memory. He pondered upon it for some time. He wondered what was happening within him. He felt his heart rate rising; he felt anxious. He was not a doctor and therefore could not determine what was happening inside his body. He decided if the occurrence repeated itself, he would tell Margaret that he had chosen to go the emergency room.

As he lay in his bed on top of the pink sheet, he felt fear—the kind that any human being feels who comes to the end of the life. He wondered if this was it. He had attended many prayer meetings for the sake of his wife. She was the one to continually encourage him. In all veracity, she had the conviction that God could cure him. She believed, so he tried to believe, but not with his whole heart. He had a rational point of view.

Whenever he would attain a state of conviction, he always wondered, *Why believe if I cannot prove?*

He encouraged the operation because some of them were successful, and he felt there was a concreteness in the procedure that he could understand. He could not fathom God's power, and that always left him with a feeling of dependency. He was the only being who made him feel that way. He could not fathom God's wonders, and he struggled— struggled with the fear that God would not heal him. He had received many messages from church members that stated, "God wants to heal you, but you must believe."

Yes, indeed, he had to believe to receive God's grace. Yes, it was grace that he sought. He felt his heart had hardened; he felt undignified. He began to feel his pride arise. *But I am a man of reason*, he thought. *I am one who must see to believe.* He continued to repeat this to himself. It made him feel justified. It made him feel righteous in his carnal thought.

He shifted his head on the pillow and tried to shake the thought out of his mind. He tried to sleep at that very moment, and he yearned for consolation, but it was nowhere to be found.

He lay there, staring at the walls, in a continual state of loneliness. He could call Margaret, but her words could never fill the emptiness he felt within. He was empty, and that hurt him more than his critical condition.

Margaret entered the room and sat on the side of the bed. "Antoine, I feel it in my heart to discuss an important issue with you," she said. "Do you know of anyone you might have wronged? Take some time to think on this, honey." Her tone indicated her utter desperation.

"No, no one at all. I am at peace with all people. I stay away from those who do not like me. I do not believe that I have done any harm to anyone in Haiti."

"I know that you had some dislike for Amidase. Would you like to call her and tell her you're sorry for anything that you might have done to her that you were not quite aware of?"

"I have done nothing wrong, Margaret. She should be telling me that she is sorry. You understand that I am her uncle. She should revere me."

"I know, Antoine, but—"

"I do not see why I should call her and say sorry." He did not understand why he should humble himself before someone without a clear reason, but finally, with a look of discontent, he said, "All right."

"You must do it now, Antoine," Margaret insisted.

He could tell that it meant a lot to her. Her gestures suggested it, and the way she paced around the room confirmed it.

He took out his phone and dialed Amidase's number. As he tapped each number, he kept asking himself why. He was operating without reason. This was new to him; he had never operated in such fashion.

"Hello."

"Hello, this is Antoine"

"Hey, Uncle" Amidase said cheerfully.

"Amidase, I am calling to tell you I'm sorry for any wrong that I have committed … against … you." He felt his voice become shaky.

"It's all right, Uncle. You haven't done me any wrong."

Antoine turned to his wife to show that he was right. He knew he had not done anything wrong. This was not the cause of his affliction. There was something else that he was not aware of.

"Antoine, I think your extended family might be involved in this," Margaret told him.

With a sudden movement, he turned toward Margaret and said, "My family loves me, Margaret. They would never do anything to hurt me. I have sacrificed a lot of my life for them; they would never do me wrong. Besides, it would be irrational for them to do anything that would put me in harm's way."

Many church friends had suggested the same thing, but they lacked proof, even common sense. He was confounded and wondered why he let some of them pray for him sometimes. Some said that it was a revelation from God, yet he had many questions. His established facts rose in his head whenever he heard such statements.

"My family would never hurt me," he reiterated. "That's impossible. It's heresy."

"Is there anyone with whom you personally had an issue?" Margaret asked.

Antoine knew she wanted him to do it as a way of liberating himself—not as a way to belittle himself before others. Nevertheless, his reasoning told him to answer no.

Of course, he had issues with many people. One, in particular, was a gospel group director. He had worked with him for many years and had many works that were to be published. After the group separated, he wanted to publish the works personally, but Matt, the choir director, would not permit it. Antoine was angry about Matt's decision, and he had a great feud with him; nevertheless, he felt righteous in his actions. He had the right to do the things he did. He did not have to ask for forgiveness—at least, he thought that he didn't.

"No!" he said, and his powerful assertion indicated the questions were enough. He turned over and attempted to sleep.

CHAPTER 16

THE DECISION

"I've decided to go to Haiti," Antoine announced. "I will be leaving next week."

Margaret sat in the car and sobbed silently. She was surprised that Antoine had made such a decision without discussing it with her. It was not the first time he had done something like that, but it never had involved an issue that was as large as the one at hand.

"Mark will pick me up and drop me off at the airport," he continued.

It appeared to Margaret that he was oblivious to her feelings. It was as if he was a computer, programmed to deliver the message. She thought of her relationship with Antoine—how fractured it had become in the last few months. Surely there was an issue in their relationship. He had already made arrangements and had his brother pay for the ticket, all without her knowledge. Margaret felt that Uncle Mark had greatly disrespected her by doing all of that behind her back.

"How could he consent to buy tickets for an unwarranted departure?"

That was a question she planned to address later. This moment required one question—why?

"I believe that I will get the medical help I need. Also, I hope to go to a church that will grant my deliverance."

Margaret knew his reasons were faulty. The lack of truth in his statements was evident. She could see how he tried to say the words that would ease her emotional pain. He knew she had a great conviction in God so he spoke of visiting a church.

She thought of losing him. She felt like she had reached the end of the line. She had been fighting the cancer battle with him for quite some time; now, it felt as if the battle was lost.

"You're not going back to Haiti, Antoine," Margaret replied, hoping to sound authoritative. Yet she knew she could not prevail. She knew her husband—once he made up his mind, no one could change it. She tried to find his reason for his decision, yet she could not find none.

"Have you told Paul?"

"No, not yet," he replied.

Caroline was too young. She would not understand this at her age. Margaret did not want to involve her.

"All right. You are an adult. The decision is in your hands. Nevertheless, I strongly recommend that you do not go to Haiti. If there is an emergency, the hospital at Gonaives will not be able to address your dire needs."

Margaret dropped Antoine at their church meeting and returned home. Upon arrival, she noticed Ms. Norma in the apartment building's hallway and felt compelled to speak to her. Ms. Norma had been Margaret's prayer partner. They always prayed together about issues they faced in their daily lives.

"I don't know why Antoine has chosen to leave, Norma. This is unbelievable to me."

"It is because of his family," Ms. Norma said. "They are directing the things he does. He speaks to them much more than he speaks to you. He is open with them. They give him advice and he listens to them. You know that, Margaret."

Margaret could feel the truth in her words. "I know your view of this is correct, Ms. Norma. He hardly leaves his phone. The other day, when he saw me enter his room, he told his brother to hang up because I had entered. I believe that his condition has reached this point because he fails to listen to me."

"I know, Margaret. God has revealed to him that some of his family members are responsible for his current health condition, yet he resists believing. He trusts them too much. He loves them too much. I have many reasons to believe that he loves them much more than you."

"You are absolutely right, Ms. Norma. Our relationship is not present anymore. I have never given up on a fight before, but I seem to be doing so now. He fails to understand that men are men. They can commit evil acts, regardless of their relationship to someone they know."

Margaret felt compelled to share the news with people who perhaps could stop Antoine. She could not believe that this was actually happening. This was the man she loved most dearly. They had shared so many close moments together. He was once her best friend; now, he seemed to be vanishing in plain sight.

She wanted to share the disheartening news with her sisters. The one she felt that she could reach out to at the present moment was Cheline.

"Cheline, have you heard of Antoine's decision?" Margaret asked.

"What decision?" Cheline replied on the other end of the phone line.

"He's told me he is going to Haiti, Cheline." Margaret said, her voice low and full of despair.

There was a slight pause. Margaret wondered how Cheline would respond. She knew Cheline as a very brave woman, but when the situation demanded tears, she would utter a cry of despair.

"Let him," Cheline answered with an emotionless voice. It was a voice that told Margaret that everything would be all right—despite any decision Antoine made. It was unexpected; it was sought—yet unexpected.

"If he desires to leave, let him. He is aware of the insufficient aid in Haiti. He is aware that his chances of dying will be increased. He doesn't listen, Margaret; he doesn't listen. Let him make his decision. You must not let his sickness take your life or your children's lives. I'm aware that Paul has been in profound distress since Antoine became ill. I've noticed the deprivation of happiness in all of your eyes. God giveth; God taketh away. Let his name be glorified."

Cheline was right. Margaret had to give up on him. Many a time she had spoken to him and advised him, yet he still walked in his self-righteous ways.

From that moment, she knew that Antoine no longer existed. She knew that he was one of the many who counted the weeks and perhaps days of their lives. She lowered herself to the carpet and leaned against the white walls of the living room. She panted, attempting to breath. It was as if the air became deprived of its oxygen.

"Live on, Margaret. You hear me? You must live on."

Margaret picked up her strength, stood up, and raised her hands to

God. She thanked him for everything. She looked at the table to see where her Bible lay. She did not see it at first, but then she found it on a small table on the patio. She opened it and read her devotions. The Word gave her strength. The scriptures were the foundation of her beliefs.

Many a time prior, she had been angry with God. She had said, "Lord, you gave me this man to be my husband. It was not foretold to me that he would be dying. Lord, you never told me this was involved."

She recalled the many moments when she had been troubled in spirit, body, and mind. She was confused but only in mind. She was angry; she felt as if almighty God was responsible for the suffering and hardship that her husband was enduring, not because he caused it but because he had the power to change it.

She wanted to ask the questions that many who had gone through hardships had asked. "Why me? Why must there be evil to those who serve God? Why must he die?" There were many other questions. She remembered the moments when she had pleaded with God, saying, "God, if you heal him, I will do great things for your glory."

As she sat on the patio and viewed the landscape, she remembered when she would say, "Lord, please heal him. Even if you don't do it for him, do it for my sake. Do it because I have been a faithful servant to you. Do it because I trust in you and have the conviction that you are able. Do it because I acknowledge that you are the God who heals. Lord, let him have my faith."

This was the most unique struggle she had undergone. All of her major requests to God were usually answered. She could not stop recalling the days when she had thought that God had stopped answering the pleas of the afflicted. Without a doubt, she was confused, and she knew it.

She tried to lock the memory of those days in a prison in her mind. "*I shall not think of those days!*" she said to herself.

Those were the most troublesome times. Despite all of the fear and doubt, she remembered when God sent people her way to help her stay faithful in the struggle. She remembered the many friends who spent entire days with her to help her with the tasks at hand. God was ever present. She doubted because she was confused. Yes, she doubted because she was confused.

❧

CHAPTER 17

THE LAST SHOW

One evening, as Antoine was sitting in his chair, he got a call from a familiar number. It was Mr. Bernel. He was someone that he had grown up with in Haiti. They were longtime friends; entertainment was something they loved.

"Antoine, would you like to host our soiree? I know that you are currently going through some tough times so it's your call."

Antoine was not feeling well, but as he approached his last days, he felt it was necessary to leave his mark in the world. "I'll be there. I will need you to provide transportation for the event."

"Your service is greatly appreciated, Antoine. I will be at your house at 5:30 p.m."

"Merci," he replied; then he hung up the phone. Margaret could not know of this. She would not permit it, he knew, but he had to do it. It was necessary, it was paramount, and it could strengthen his legacy.

He got up from his bed with a great effort and went to his closet. There were three shirts that he loved in particular for these performances. Next to his yellow glittering shirt was his silver shirt. It shone in the light in a very appealing way. It was appropriate for the occasion—he wanted the attention to be on him. He wanted every eye to follow his movements, every ear to listen to his words, and every hand to applaud his short discourses. He was eloquent, and he desired that everyone in Palm Beach County would know it—at least every Haitian American. He had devoted a lot of his time to learning the French language and he had mastered.

It was every Haitian's desire to hear French spoken at its finest at a social event.

On the day of the event, he felt he could not hide it from his wife. As she sat on the patio, as she did on most days, he approached her and spoke the words that he knew she would abhor.

"Margaret, I want you to know that I will be hosting a Protestant church's anniversary."

"What?"

He held his hands in his pockets and bowed his head. He was not happy that he'd hidden this from Margaret until the very end, but it had to be done. Too many questions would have arisen and she would have attempted to stop him.

"Antoine, you know you cannot go. You might not be able to handle it physically. It might be too strenuous for you. Even managing some of your tasks here can be difficult at times. I strongly ask that you can cancel it."

"Margaret, it is too late. I have already given them my word. I will fulfill that which my mouth has spoken. Besides, the concert is tonight. I cannot cancel it now."

"Antoine, I worry for you, yet you seem to not take that into consideration. Don't you want to live?"

He did not know how to answer that question. He was looking beyond that point. He was looking at the world at a time after he would be gone, but his name would forever remain—at least in the Haitian community.

"Listen, if the pain becomes unbearable, I will ask them to transport me to a local hospital. If, at any time, I feel like it is too strenuous, I will ask them to bring me home."

"All right, it is your decision. You are an adult. I trust that you can wisely decide for yourself."

◦❧◦

"Hello, is this Antoine?"

"Yes," he responded.

"I have arrived at Marina Bay, but I am not sure where you are."

"Go straight toward the office. It is that smaller building. Once you have reached the office, make a left, then continue down the pathway. You will see me in a silver shirt."

"All right, you may come out now."

"I will be all right, Margaret. It's only for a few hours." He hung up his phone and walked toward the door.

When he first got outside, he did not notice the car that had arrived for him. Across from him were many parked cars. He walked down the sidewalk and finally noticed a red car. He waved, hoping that the driver would acknowledge him. Sure enough, he did. The car came toward him, but just before the car stopped, he heard Paul call out from behind him.

"Wait, Dad! I have your piano for you."

"Yes, thank you, son," Antoine responded as his son placed the miniature instrument in the trunk of the man's car.

What a great child, Antoine thought, acknowledging Paul's effort. With not much time left, he opened the door and sat down.

"How are you doing, Antoine?" Vens asked.

"I'm all right. How many people will be there?"

"A couple of thousand. People are flying out of New York and many faraway states to visit this. Some have even traveled internationally to be here. Our pastor is quite well known and many would like to come to support the great accomplishments that our church has made in past years."

"That's good," Antoine replied. To him, the number of the people was quite pleasing. He took consolation in that and tried to dismiss the pain he had already begun to feel.

⁂

"Tonight, we have a special guest. I have known him very well for all of my life. We were raised together. He speaks French in a very vibrant way. Ladies and gentlemen, please welcome Antoine Darius."

Antoine stood up and waved in a fashion that resembled that of a president. With an alpha-male walk, he made his way to the stage, elated that he soon would give a speech. "Good evening, ladies and gentlemen," he said with an air of pride. "I am Antoine, as stated by my dear friend Dr. Harton. Tonight, we celebrate the anniversary of this great church, pastored by Dr. James Saintilus." He paused, patiently allowing the crowd to applaud his statements and allowing them to reach a state of euphoria as they gave honor to the pastor and partially to themselves.

With an increased surge of enthusiasm, he said, "To commence with the celebration, I would like to introduce our greatly admired singer, Pedro Halerie." Antoine clapped his hands, initiating the action that the constituents in the assembly followed.

Antoine did not know Pedro Halerie, but he had heard that he was a great singer, and from the people's applause, he was certain that assessment was true.

In an admirable fashion, he gently placed the microphone into Pedro's hand and gave him a quick yet noticeable hug. It was part of his custom; many people felt more comfortable with certain gestures. To Antoine, it made the concert more genuine.

In the distance, he noticed an obscure corridor, from which he could observe the performer and the audience. He walked over to it and began to reflect. *How much was I acknowledged? Was my walk confident? Did I properly address my audience? How complex should my language be?*

His examination was thorough. It was one of many he had conducted to improve his craft and attain a state of perfection at every event. Finally, he decided that his words had been were adequate and relevant.

Looking upward, he noticed the luminous lights. Looking toward the audience, he beheld the many seats occupied by many people. They were on their feet, dancing, clapping, cheering. Their actions suggested perfect happiness—assuming that existed. They were all in a state of illusion, Antoine decided, one that would last for the remaining two hours. Afterward, each individual would return to his or her own interpretation of reality. Some would have theirs occupied with happiness and others with grief, perhaps even unbearable grief. He was in the latter category, but as he stood there, in that dark corner, in that gloomy state, he tried to renew his state of mind, for he was a man with a purpose—the sole purpose of growing his legacy. His name was known among many, yet he was not satisfied. He wanted to attain new heights.

He continued with his eloquent introductions and interjections. The sound in the room was mostly the applause he personally received. He knew it was for him, for it was noticeable whenever he walked on stage.

Glancing at their expressions, Antoine could see the sincerity of their enjoyment.

"The next performer—" Everyone clapped. He smiled. "Thank you, thank you." He had not finished his sentence, yet the people cheered. He found great comfort in that. When people acknowledged him for what he thought of himself, that gave him the greatest satisfaction.

"Merci, merci," he finally said and concluded the concert.

Feeling unable to linger with audience any longer, he exited the building by a back door. When he arrived at the car, many people begin to surround him, thanking him for the fabulous job that he had done. Some even asked for his phone number—and he gave it to them without hesitation. Yet he earnestly felt that this would be his last public performance. With the condition of his health and the degrading stages it attained each day, he sincerely believed he had reached the end of his career as a host.

"I have heard about you, Antoine, but I never knew that you were so eloquent," a women from the audience commented.

Antoine remained silent; he did not know how to respond. He often had heard that comment. Once on the highway, he recognized that the cars moved at a great speed. *Life as well moves at a great speed,* he thought. He was only in his midlife, yet the truth dawned upon him. In times past, he would leave the concerts with a liveliness reflected his sturdiness; now, he took comfort in the soft feeling the chairs had and in the images his mind had captured.

The images flashed in front of him, each composed of a smiling individual and hands that were clapping.

"Margaret, can you please send Paul outside for a minute," Antoine said into his phone.

Without granting her a chance to reply, he hung up the phone. He did not want to speak; he wanted to be left alone. Even breathing now seemed to demand a great amount of energy.

"Thank you once again, Antoine," Vens, the driver, said. "Your performance meant a lot to us. It will be greatly remembered."

Antoine nodded, gave a quick smile, and then asked Paul to get his electronic keyboard.

Upon entering the house, he saw Margaret awaiting his arrival. It was in her nature to make sure that her husband came home at his appointed time.

Without approaching her, he gave her a look of acknowledgement and entered his room. There were not many words they could have exchanged. Antoine felt that Margaret could not understand his purpose, his reason. Her wisdom contradicted his common sense; nevertheless, his wife was always right.

The concert had been strenuous, and it was difficult to finish, but he had concluded it. The people always remembered the individuals who concluded the show.

He felt a sense of happiness at arriving home, but a sadness occupied his mind because of his condition. Without changing his garments, he stacked two pillows on the bed and lay his head on them. He wanted to facilitate his respiration and sleep. With a last sigh, he entered the state of unconsciousness.

CHAPTER 18

DEPARTURE

Paul sat on his piano stool and played the last stanza of Chopin's saddest classical piece, Prelude op. 28, no. 4. He let the himself feel the musical vibrations that the tonic chord emitted as he stroked it. He inhaled, held in his breath, then slowly exhaled. He quietly moved his stool and walked to his father's room. On his way there, he noticed a tie on a chair. It was not his, so he assumed it was his father's. He took the tie and folded it in half and quietly opened the door to Antoine's room.

These days, most noise caused great frustration to Antoine, unless he anticipated it. Knowing this, Paul stepped quietly. Antoine was awake and had a pair of earbuds in his ears. He seemed troubled and appeared to be deep in thought. It was not an uncommon sight, yet that day, it was different.

Paul attached the tie to a white plastic hanger. He wondered about the cause of his father's troubled face.

"Paul, I have decided to leave the country. I believe that I will get my spiritual healing in Haiti, and if anything happens, I will receive medical care."

Paul knew that his father was leaving; his mom had told him. Paul assumed that his father had come to the conclusion of telling Paul himself. Even so, Paul found himself startled by the news. "Come on, Dad. You know very well that the Lord God almighty can heal you here. If you still lack faith, it will not go well with you in Haiti." He waited for a response from his dad but none came. He stood there for thirty seconds longer, but by then, his father had focused his attention on his phone screen. Paul knew his father was not asking for advice. Still, he hoped that his dad would change his mind—but that was not to be the case.

At 5:48 p.m., Margaret entered their little apartment with one suitcase and many bags in her hands. Some bags contained clothes but mostly undergarments. Paul got up from the couch and helped his mom arrange the clothing.

"Make sure you eat only natural foods," she said to Antoine.

He nodded in response. He was not in the mood to talk. These days were the silent days; he hardly spoke to anyone. He dwelled on his reasoning in his head. Yet his nodding was sufficient for Margaret; Paul could see it on her face. She did not have the capacity to hide displeasure. She expressed it with her face and her voice.

Paul watched his mother neatly pack the clothes and the toiletries that Antoine might need. In the right corner of the suitcase, she stacked some undergarments; to the left, some boxers; in the center, a portable stove. In the lower right corner, she arranged the natural protein supplements that were specifically ordered for Antoine. Finally, she placed a Bible and a hymnbook in the outer pocket so that he could reach it easily whenever he desired.

A short time later, Aunt Cicie entered the apartment. "Antoine, why are leaving? You must not leave," she said.

"I will come back," Antoine replied. "I will come back."

His words seemed to resonate in the room. They were hopeful words. They were words that pleased their ears.

"I believe you," Cicie replied as she pulled a chair to sit. They discussed the arrangements, particularly the financial aspect of the trip. He had already paid for the tickets and all other provisional costs. Even though that was the truth, everyone wanted to be sure.

It was 6:52 p.m. when Uncle Mark arrived. He was expected but not welcome—at least not by Paul, Margaret, and Caroline. He was going to take Antoine away. When Uncle Mark got there, Antoine was dressed and sitting patiently in a chair. Margaret had prepared much food beforehand, and it was on the table for them to eat. Uncle Mark sat at the end of the table and spoke to everyone. The conversation was happy; nothing troubling that would increase the tension that was already in the room.

Grandpa Pradere arrived but decided not to eat. He believed that one must not eat on certain occasions—that was one of his ideals, and Paul respected him greatly for it. Within a short time during the dinner, some of them laughed, although Paul knew it was not genuine laughter. Rather, it was the type of laughter that people do in order to escape the reality of certain truths.

"He will be OK. Nothing wrong will happen," Uncle Mark said to Margaret. The others were in their own conversations so only Paul and Margaret heard Uncle Mark. Paul was sure of that because there were no reactions.

Margaret seemed to ignore his comments and proceeded with her meal. She seemed tired of the situation.

When everyone finished eating, Paul got the suitcases and helped Uncle Mark place them in the trunk of his white SUV.

Antoine and his family exchanged no words for there was none to be exchanged. Paul had reached the point of hopelessness and decided not to cry for anything that might come to pass.

Paul went to the door and opened it for his father.

"Goodbye, everyone," Antoine said as he left the house on a journey from which he was uncertain he would return. As Paul shut the door behind them, Antoine said, "Can you come here, please?"

Paul was not sure why his dad wanted him, but being an obedient son, he walked toward his father, oblivious to what might come next. Before he had time to think much of his dad's actions, Antoine pulled Paul toward him and hugged his son to his chest. It was a gesture Paul had not experienced from his father for a long time. He was stuck there, unwilling to move, and confused, perhaps even shocked. The experience was surreal; it was the wish he had written in his letter. At that very moment, he felt his prayers were answered. He did not know how to cherish the act; he had become emotionless and didn't know how to respond. He shut the car door for his dad and went back inside.

CHAPTER 19

FINAL DAYS

"Are you sure about this?" Antoine asked as his brother lectured him.

"You know I am right Antoine. Going back to your native land is the best choice for you."

Antoine supposed his brother was right. He was dying, and there was no chance for him to turn back. The disease had not only consumed his liver but also his soul. His respiration was labored most of the time, he asked for water more often, and he felt pain at a greater degree. He wanted to leave the United States so that the burden of his death would not be too heavy for his wife. The cost of burial in Haiti was much less, relative to that of America. He didn't want to be a financial burden. His family had tried to help him so much, but there was nothing that could be done at this stage. Antoine had given up on God. All hope was lost.

The last time he'd gone to the hospital, one of the nurses had asked if he had written his will. He was shocked because he was hoping that he would be cured. At that moment, his hope in humanity died. It was a losing battle.

On the airplane, he thought of heaven, the place that he hoped he would be when he died.

"I want to stay in Port-au-Prince for some time," he told his brother Barius as he entered his car.

"That's all right."

He wanted to visit church one last time. He wanted to know if the Lord had any revelations for him. On the day of the church service, Cassandra, a dear friend of his, came to take him there. On the way, he tried to stay silent. It was hard for him to speak; his organs' functions had diminished greatly.

"How are you holding up, Antoine?" Cassandra asked.

"I'm hanging in there," he responded.

They entered the white-painted building and found a seat among those who had come for deliverance. During the service, someone spoke of someone being sick as a result of a family member's actions. Those were the same words Antoine had heard in America. He could not believe his ears. God continually told him the cause of his ailment, but he had failed to believe.

At the conclusion of the service, he asked to go to Gonaives, the city where he had lived for his entire life.

On the day of his departure, he took his belongings and waited patiently for Barius in his room.

"It's time, Antoine. We must leave," Barius said. Barius took Antoine's luggage and carried it to the trunk of the car for him.

As Antoine went down the stairs, he leaned on the handrails and gently took even steps. He did not want his movements to feel too strenuous.

With shallow, irregular breathing, Antoine entered the car and rested on the seat. His brother exchanged no words with him. There wasn't any communication whatsoever. Antoine felt as if he was left alone to perish.

When he arrived at his home, no one was waiting for him. *This is strange*, he thought. He remembered the days when his return from any trip was the joy of his extended family. He mustered his courage and entered the room that his wife and he once shared. Opening a drawer in one of the nightstands, he found an album containing pictures that were relevant to his life. He beheld Paul hugging his sister in one of them. In another, he saw his wife, Margaret, standing with Paul near a gate. They had smiles on their faces—that gave him some consolation.

Within two hours, the house was occupied. Everyone entered and went to attend to their daily tasks. It was as if Antoine's existence was no longer significant. He began to wonder why they acted in such a manner. Then, at that very moment, it dawned on him that he was only valued because of the work he did for them. They had cherished him because he had sacrificed his life for them. Now, however, he was deficient. He had lost his capabilities, and therefore, no one came to see how he was doing.

Unable to assuage his emotional pain, he took his phone and dialed Cassandra's number. "Cassandra, I need you to retrieve me from my house as soon as possible," he said and then hung up. He did not wait for her reply; he just wanted to leave his family's presence.

By the second week, he was living miles away from his home. He was bedridden, a state that he strongly considered to be deplorable. He thought of the words that Margaret had said about his ailment, and he acknowledged that she was right. "Margaret told me so," he said quietly.

"She told you what?" Cassandra inquired as she brought new linens to his room.

He did not respond. There was nothing to say.

"What have I done to deserve this?" he bellowed. Then, he gave up the ghost.

CHAPTER 20

THE DEMISE

It was 11:12 p.m. when Margaret got the phone call. Paul sat at his piano, playing a sorrowful song. Margaret told him that Antoine was no longer responding and appeared to be dead.

At that very moment, Margaret knew that was it. She knew that the man she had known for all her life now was deceased. She knew that the only man to whom she'd ever said the words *I love you* was deceased. She knew that, at that particular moment, she had become a widow. She didn't need any further confirmation. She knew that Antoine had perished. She could no longer hold the tears; she had to let go. She could no longer display any courage, and she faltered. She could no longer display her resilience; she was broken. "God gives, and God takes away. Let his name be glorified."

As Paul fixed his eyes on his mother, he noticed the magnitude of her conviction in God. She did not curse God for the loss; rather, she gave glory to his name. His grandfather attempted to console her, giving her pats on the back to let her know that she was not alone, that she was not forgotten and always would have them.

Paul resumed playing his song. He was not shocked; he knew it would happen eventually, and the time had come for him to move on. He always had hope, although he knew from the start that it was in vain. Antoine had lacked the conviction that would have preserved his life. Paul knew that; Margaret knew it also, but she did not want to believe it. In a way, they all tried to defy the Word. Every single person who was healed in the scriptures received that healing because he or she had faith and believed that the Lord God almighty was real and was able to perform miracles. Antoine never could believe that. He resolved to living by his carnal reasonings, and he perished.

Paul felt anger, not at God but at Antoine for failing to accept God's grace. He was furious. He had hoped that he would tell many how God had healed his father from stage IV cancer, but that was not the case. His father had failed him. He could not cry for such a man. He wanted to cry, but his anger prevented that. He had done everything in his power to help his father, yet this had happened. If he refused God's grace, how could he then expect Paul to mourn for him?

"Paul, get off the piano," Grandpa Pradere said.

"No, leave him. The music helps him express his sorrow," Margaret responded in Paul's defense.

"No, he needs to get off and think of what has happened. I also suggest he drink some coffee. It will help to get through it.

There is no more sorrow, Paul thought. *I did all I could. My father never listened to the advice we gave him, and his foolishness led to his demise.* Paul knew it was sad, not because his father had died but because of all the sorrow that he had caused for so many people. *If he did not believe in prayers, then why did he let us pray for him?*

Paul knew that he had to respect his mother's feelings, so he kept his thoughts to himself. He even affected a distressed face. He did not want anyone to detect his anger. He had to help his mother. "It's OK, Mom. God will take care of us," Paul reassured her.

Of course, God always had taken care of him and his mother. The Almighty always had done his job. God was the only being who had never given up on Paul. By God's grace, Paul acknowledged that his father's demise was not a result of God's inaction but rather a result of man giving up on God. When people give up on God, very bad things happen.

Paul stayed in the living room with his mom, attempting to console her, but he could not assuage the anger that was coursing through him. He made a promise to himself to never cry for his father's demise. God had wanted to help him, and he simply said no by not believing.

Paul continued to feel angry. Those who knew the story and wanted to see whether God was capable of healing would stay in their disbelief because Paul did not have the opportunity to testify to God's healing in Antoine's life.

Apart from being a professor, Antoine had been a musician at church. He had come to church every Sunday and played for the congregation to glorify God. Now, he was dead because of disbelief. *What a loss*, Paul thought. *What was his motive for playing in church? Was it to glorify God, or was it for self-gratification? Was it for the sole acknowledgement of society?* These questions ran through Paul's mind.

Tired of acting, Paul made his way to the couch and took a nap. Not one tear ran down his face.

During the next few days, many family members and church members came to give their condolences. They were very nice. Paul remembered many of their faces as they hugged his mom. *What a sight*, he thought.

Whenever too many people came at once, Paul would withdraw to the patio. He felt uncomfortable around too many people expressing sympathy. He had not received much emotion from his father, and he was unsure of how to perceive it.

He noticed they comforted his mother with monetary gifts. He was happy that they expressed sincere care. He could see that their actions reflected those of Jesus Christ.

"Margaret, we have to buy the tickets for the flight to the funeral," Niclaire said. He was a family friend and he was one of the people that cared deeply about Margaret.

"I know. I will need some time to get things in order first. Call Uncle Charles. Tell him we will be arriving next week," Margaret answered.

Niclaire went outside to make the phone call.

In the meantime, Aunt Cheline entered the house to visit Margaret. She approached Margaret with a strong and supportive look on her face and gestured in a manner that indicated everything would be all right. "The world is not over. Now, take courage and continue raising your children," she boldly said. "I want to take Paul shopping in preparation for the funeral. I know that you're someone who usually does not ask for favors, but we would really like to do this."

"That's fine," Margaret said.

"Paul, let's go. Pachum is waiting outside for us," Cheline said.

As Paul left the house, Cheline patted his back to console him.

Paul had to suppress his desire to laugh. He had lost his humanism, but they had yet to know it. "I'm fine," he finally said.

When he entered their car, he saw Leny, his cousin, and his brother sitting in the back seat. Paul could tell they felt sad for him. *Aww*, he thought, *they actually care.* He appreciated their sympathy, but he wanted to tell them that that he was all right. He wanted to remind them that things occur in life that are beyond their control. This was the truth. Instead, he quietly said, "Hey, guys."

"Hey, Paul," they replied.

They did not have the courage to say anything else to him. They'd never had a cousin who lost a parent. This was new to them; they'd never had to show sympathy for a death.

Paul shook Pachum's hand in greeting. As he did, Pachum drew Paul closer to him to strengthen him. "Be strong for your mom," Pachum said.

"You are now the man of the house," Cheline added. "Make sure everything is in order. If you ever need anything, always know that you have us."

When they arrived at the mall, Paul led them to the clothing department. After a while, he noticed a slim dark suit that seemed appropriate for the occasion. "I have found the suit. I'll be in the dressing room," he said. He wanted to be sure they knew where he was.

He removed the jacket and the pants from the hanger and put them on. He looked at himself in the mirror and thought of the man he had become. The dark color of the suit seemed to reflect the color of his soul. "Give me a heart of flesh and not of stone," he prayed.

The following day, his mom received a call from Julian at around ten o'clock in the morning. Paul became concerned; he wanted to know why she had called. As he approached his mother, he could hear Julian say, "Margaret, I'm so sorry. I am so sorry. Please forgive me, Margaret. Please forgive me.".

Margaret stayed quiet; she did not dare respond. She wondered why Julian had begged for forgiveness. Nevertheless, it did not take Margaret much time to realize that Julian was somehow involved in Antoine's death.

Paul could not believe what he'd overheard. He knew that Julian was somehow involved, but he'd only had theories until then. Now, he was unbelievably shaken. *Sorry for what?* he thought. *Sorry because you allowed*

*your greed to cause you to act in an envious way? Sorry because what you had
expected did not come to pass?*

Margaret and her children were still alive. Was Julian sorry because
she had undermined the wondrous power of God?

Paul smiled. He knew there would be repercussions. Now, all he had to
do was wait. He had never forgotten that his God executed righteousness
and that he judged with equity. This was Paul's truth.

Approximately eighty-six hours after Antoine's death, Julian's daughter
called Margaret on the phone. At the time, Paul was working on his
schoolwork, and Margaret was cooking.

When the phone rang, Paul retrieved it from his mother's brown purse
and ran to Margaret. He did not want to answer, but he saw on caller ID
that it was Julian's daughter, Hailey, calling.

"Margaret, Julian could not leave her brother behind," Hailey said.
"She has just died." She gave Margaret some time to absorb the information
and then said, "She had been experiencing diarrhea, and this morning,
when I came in, I found her dead on the bathroom floor."

Margaret could not believe her ears. She began to pace the floor.

"I want to make sure her funeral is in Haiti as well. I was wondering
whether I could do it with Antoine's funeral. I feel that it's necessary that
we do it in their provincial hometown."

"No, Hailey, I cannot permit that. My husband's funeral will be in
Gonaives in his church. That is the plan that I originally had, and that
is the plan I will keep," Margaret replied assertively. She did not have to
consent to this request from his extended family. Antoine's immense love
for them had greatly contributed to his demise. Margaret had fought very
hard for his survival, but human beings do not always get what they desire.

"All right," Hailey responded and hung up the phone.

ॐ

CHAPTER 21

BACK HOME

It had been seven years since Paul had been to Haiti. He had formed beautiful memories there. Upon his arrival at the Port-au Prince airport, he noticed Uncle Mark at a distance. He waved to greet him. Before Antoine's demise, Paul would have run to his uncle and jumped on him to express his love unto him. Now, times had changed, and circumstances had changed.

Paul knew that Uncle Mark was aware of the cause of Antoine's death and that he never stood for the righteous cause. He wanted to love, but he acted as though the word was too strong for him to express. He waved back in response. Paul wondered whether he really cared.

"Paul, I want you to retrieve our luggage from the baggage area," his mother said.

What if I can't find it? he thought. He felt frustrated. He had just lost his father, which potentially destabilized his entire home.

During the trip to Gonaives, he noticed shirtless men attempting to cool themselves in the intense heat. Paul loved his country, but it needed serious help.

When they finally arrived at Gonaives, he greeted everyone and then went to sit on the roof of their residential building. Haiti was like that; many of the homes had access to their rooftops.

When night approached, Paul heard church hymns being sung by Christians in a nearby church. He then thought of God's marvelous grace and of all the mercy he had bestowed. Paul thought of the many ways that God had ensured his survival. He was nothing but grateful.

On the morrow, Uncle Charles approached him with a serious

expression. "Paul, I want you to know that you have to give a speech on behalf of Antoine. You must speak of what he meant to you and how you perceived him."

After hearing the request, Paul thought profoundly of how he had perceived his father. He thought of the many days when he had worked hard when he was in America. As positive as he wanted his thoughts to be, however, he could not remove the memories of the many days he had been emotionally deprived. He recalled the short conversations with his father when he had sought long ones. He remembered the many times his dad would spend hours on the phone, talking to his extended family in Haiti but never think of speaking to him. He remembered the pain he felt. He remembered the wishes he wrote in the letter and that they had hardly been granted. He recalled every single moment of it.

Now, for the sake of society, he would have to fabricate some nice words in order to show that he "genuinely" loved his father. Well, perhaps he did truly love him, and perhaps his dad had felt the same, but Paul struggled to believe that because his father did not express it in the ways that Paul sought. He had longed for cuddles and hugs, not just the simple greetings.

He took a pen started to write the draft.

My father was a man of reason, one who believed in education and one who sacrificed a lot for the well-being of his family.

Those were the first words he wrote. That sentence alone embodied how he saw Antoine.

One evening, while everyone sat on the patio of Aunt Rossette's house, a man approached the stairs, and Paul realized it was Barius. The closer he got, the greater Paul's resentment became.

"Hello, everyone," Barius said, as if it would mask his mischievous heart and make him more appealing.

Before Barius could notice Paul's presence, Paul excused himself and went to the guest room. He lay on the bed as he attempted to withdraw from the reality that his uncle sat just beyond the room's wall.

"Where's Paul?" Barius asked, as if he really wanted to know of his well-being.

Paul knew that Barius was involved in the conspiracy. He knew Barius was partly responsible for his father's demise. He did not want to greet him or come near him in a way that might indicate a sense of love.

"He's here," Uncle Charles said. "Paul, can you come out here, please? Your uncle is calling for you."

Paul pretended to be asleep. He hoped he would be left alone and that Barius wouldn't know where he was. He did not want to sit across from Uncle Barius and look in his eyes as if he was not one of the culprits. He felt a hand vigorously rubbing his feet, as if trying to wake him. He looked up and saw Uncle Charles staring at him.

"Paul, you have to go greet your uncle," he said. "You know, he is your uncle, after all. You are obliged to greet him."

Due to the respect that Paul had for Uncle Charles, he felt he had to obey; it was imperative.

When he went outside, he noticed Barius's gruesome face staring at him. At that particular moment, Paul felt a lump in his throat, as if he was about to choke. He could not swallow, inhale, or exhale. He felt his heart transformed from that of a man to that of a beast. He gave his uncle a piercing, sharp look, as if to say, "What are you doing in my presence?"

He then noticed an unusual movement. Barius extended his hand, as if to give Paul a handshake. *How strange*, Paul thought. He had given thousands of handshakes, but something about this one from Barius seemed wrong. He viewed it as if an abductor was extending his arms to grab him and potentially hurt him. He began to tremble. He stared at Barius directly in his eyes and refused to extend his hand in return.

Uncle Barius's hand was still in the air, as if he lacked the understanding that Paul did not trust him. He left it in the air, as if Paul was his beloved nephew who would never forsake him.

Is this guy serious? Paul thought. *I'm not going to pretend I like him for the sake of society. He should have convinced Julian to abort her demonic plans. He complied because he was envious and failed to stand for a righteous cause.* As far as Paul was concerned, Barius merely existed to him.

Paul noticed Barius's disbelief, but he shook his head and tilted it slightly downward, indicating that he wanted to stay away from him. Paul did not mean to be rude, but he felt that shaking Barius's hand would indicate the greatest hypocrisy.

"Shake his hand!" Uncle Mark bellowed.

"I'm sorry, Uncle, but I can't," Paul finally gathered the courage to say.

"Leave," Grandpa Pradere said, clearly irritated. "Get out of here."

As Paul walked away, Uncle Charles spanked him on his rear to express his utter disgust.

They seemed to have forgotten that emotions were concrete things that people experienced. Sometimes, that could cause one to defy established principles. It could even move one to go against the commands of authority. That was Paul's truth at that particular moment. He went back to the room and lay on the bed. He thought upon his actions to determine if they were warranted. He still had a chance to say sorry—that is, if he decided that his actions were morally culpable. He wanted to comply to their rules, but he wondered how that would define his character. He would feel weak and prone to manipulation, like a follower who could not stand firm on decisions.

Although his actions might have been socially unacceptable, he cared not. This circumstance was the exception. Besides, even if it was wrong, Barius would not be avenged. The scriptures stated that God does not avenge the wicked. Paul remembered reading such a passage.

❧

At the viewing, Paul noticed many family members he had not seen in a very long time. He saw the sympathy on their faces. He saw Julian's eldest daughter greet his mom. Before long, many people swarmed around Margaret, each with their unique words of consolation.

During the middle of the event, the man leading the service called for Margaret. She had told him that she wanted to sing a song, and now the time had come. She began to sing.

> The more the evil is pressing, the greater my misery is
> The more I take refuge, oh Jesus, in your arms
> Among all the dangers, it is you who reassures me
> Against all assaults, you are my shield
> You always give me according to my confidence
> When I asked everything, did not I receive everything?
> With you all triumph is assured
> We are sure to win; we have already won

The words were powerful, Paul began to tremble as he watched his mom sing the song with strength. She trusted in Jesus; she believed that although the circumstances were difficult, she had already won. Paul agreed with every word; he trusted in Jesus too.

Before the conclusion of the gathering, Barius approached Paul once more. He had his hand extended in the same manner as before. At that same moment, Paul thought of a biblical passage that depicted Judas's betrayal. When Jesus was speaking to his disciples and a crowd came, he already knew that he had been betrayed by Judas. Even then, he allowed Judas to greet him with a kiss. That was a profound event then, and now, his uncle had his hand extended, and Paul knew he had to extend his too. Not only that, but he had to shake it with his strength—his will. He gathered his courage and crushed the resentment he felt within himself. He shook Barius's hand and greeted his uncle. He felt relief at that moment; he felt free. It was as if he had forgiven him. Although his actions were unwarranted, he knew that the scripture stated, "Where sin abounds, grace abounds much more."

"Let's go," Uncle Charles said.

He turned and noticed his mother was gathering her belongings. He stood up and gave one last look at the people present. It was a unique sight. Not one seat was left empty. People had heard the announcement and wanted to be supportive.

Vanity, vanity, all is vanity, Paul thought. Antoine had worked very hard to be esteemed and acknowledged. Now, it was all over. Although many gathered at this event that was centered around him, Antoine could not view it.

"For the safety of us all, we must leave," Uncle Charles reminded them.

They quickly entered the car and went to their house.

They all knew that some of the members of Antoine's family practiced witchcraft against them. Now that they were in their midst, they worried that they would take their hatred to the next level and attempt to inflict physical harm.

In the house, Paul looked at his suit one last time. He thought of the song his mom would sing at the funeral. He reviewed the speech he had written. He felt ready to perform—yes, to conduct himself in a way that was socially acceptable.

~~~
⚬~

C H A P T E R 2 2

THE INTERMENT

The day had finally come when all of the sorrows would be buried—or at least should be buried.

"Paul, it is time to go," his uncle shouted. It was the same uncle who had shouted those same words before Paul had left Haiti for the very first time.

"I am coming, Uncle," he responded. He had been ready for thirty minutes. He had woken up that morning, indulged in his prayer, showered, and got dressed. While he sat and reflected, he heard an urgent call.

"Paul, you must eat!" Aunt Rossette shouted.

Man does not live on bread alone, he thought. These days, the scriptures had become the premise for his actions and thoughts.

Before he retrieved his food, he carefully positioned his dark glasses on his face. He reviewed himself in the mirror. He stood with an erect posture and noticed his emotionless face.

"Good," he said to himself.

He retrieved the food from his aunt and thanked her for it. He was pleased to savor it, yet he found it hard to swallow. It was as if his muscles had retired. He drank some water and tried again, collecting food on a spoon and placing it in his mouth. He chewed a little harder this time, but he still could not swallow the food. Still, he thought he was OK. His spirit perhaps was willing, but he supposed his body was not.

He reviewed the speech he had written. He noticed the truthful words and the words that were not parallel to his beliefs—the ones he would have to say in front of the assembly.

On the road to the church, he noticed the vast procession. So many people had gathered for Antoine's funeral.

When they entered the church, his mom and Aunt Cicie approached the casket.

"Antoine, Antoine, Antoine!" his mom yelled. She was in utter disbelief. She was shaken. She had heard that he had perished, but now she beheld it with her own eyes. She began to scream at the top of her lungs. "Antoine, you can't go now! You cannot leave us right now!"

"You were so good to us. You told me you would come back. You told me you would come back!" Aunt Cicie screamed.

Paul wanted to tell Aunt Cicie that human are limited and can't fulfill every promise. Not everything is within a human's power. Paul, however, could not afford to tell her those words. He knew he could not tell her.

As Paul approached the casket, he smelled a fragrance. Margaret had purchased a cologne for him with a distinguishable scent. He got as close as necessary to behold his father's face. He noticed the manner in which his eyelids were shut. As Paul lowered his gaze, he noticed that his father's mouth had been glued shut. It seemed remarkably disfigured; it appeared as though it had taken a triangular form. It also was also slightly folded.

Paul looked at the man he had greatly esteemed, the man who had taught him the necessity of being the best at whatever he did.

Now, he lay dead, motionless, unable to prove to others who he was, unable to satisfy the wishes of society.

The real *reality of life*, Paul thought.

The pastor came and ushered him to the second floor of the church. "You may sit here," he said. He then ushered the rest of Margaret's company to their respective seats.

With his eyes oblivious to the outside world, Paul observed the event quite profoundly. He was aware when Antoine's extended family entered the church. He noticed how they swiftly sat, wearing their nice apparel.

"We gather here today to give our last farewells to a man we greatly loved," the pastor said. "He served in this church for twenty-seven years. It was here that he was baptized. He was the leader of many departments in this church. He was intelligent, disciplined, and a hard worker."

Paul heard wailing, particularly to his far left. That was where his extended family sat. They cried as the pastor spoke.

"Antoine," they cried. "Why did you leave us?"

Oh, I know, Paul thought. *It is because you became envious and desired the death of my mom, my sister, and me. You bewitched him, thinking that it would only hurt us. Well, now your provider is dead.*

While the pastor spoke, they continued with their disturbing wailing.

"If you really loved him, why did you proceed with such demonic act?" Paul wanted to ask them.

Maestro Venice came to pulpit and introduced a song that they felt compelled to sing.

Paul could not remember the words, but he remembered that it involved leaving this earth and going to God. It was played in a minor key, and naturally had a sad and gloomy tone.

He felt to a sudden movement to his right and heard his mother give a loud, piercing cry. She proceeded to cry uncontrollably. He noticed Mr. Benson and his wife running to console her. Her agony was great; perhaps it had reached its culmination.

"Mom, it's all right," Paul reassured her, but that wasn't sufficient. He could tell from her continual and violent shaking that she had reached her breaking point.

When she finally stopped, she appeared as though everything was OK. It looked as if she had regained her strength. He was quite amazed.

She walked to pulpit and proceeded with her discourse of who Antoine was to her and to others. It was a biography of his life.

Paul knew some of the things she spoke of, but other things he did not know.

"I would like to sing a song to glorify God for enabling me to endure this hardship," she said. She gestured toward Paul; she wanted him to play the song. It was quite symbolic, as Antoine had taught him how to play.

Paul went to the piano, but his mother started singing before he could begin to play. They had practiced the song in A minor, but she was singing in a different key. Paul struggled to find that key. Margaret proceeded with the second verse, but Paul had yet to find the proper key. He glanced at the maestro for help, but it was in vain.

Finally, Paul struck a D minor chord and found it appropriate. He felt relieved and began playing the song. By that time, though, Margaret was singing the final verse. It was as if all of his music-theory lessons had gone to waste. He panicked, not knowing what to do. He left the piano in disappointment and joined his mom as she was escorted off the podium. He felt great shame; his head was bowed in agony. He simply did not know what to do.

"It's all right, brother," Mr. Benson said as he patted Paul's shoulders. He seemed to think that Paul's anguish was due to Antoine's death, but Paul was sad because he had failed to play the song the right way.

As the end of the funeral approached, the pastor's wife came and retrieved Margaret's company. She tugged at Paul's arm and gestured for him to go downstairs. He hastily went out of the church and into an alleyway. He could not believe what he saw. Many people were gathered, waiting for the hearse to transport the casket to the tomb.

He got into Uncle Charles's car and sat patiently. "Paul, you need to know where your father is buried," Uncle Charles said. "You may not come with us to the house yet."

Uncle Charles drove him to a location that was near the burial place, and Paul walked the rest of the way on foot. He saw his cousin Syndie as she passed by on a motorcycle.

"Hey, Syndie," he said.

She looked at him for a slight moment and then responded, "Hello, Paul."

No other words were exchanged for everything that had been hidden had been made known.

The burial ground was quite unique to Paul. He could see the differences in the social classes by the architectural designs of the elevated tombstones. Some of them were nicely painted, whereas some of them only had a concreted exterior. Even at the grave, people's economic status could still haunt them.

"Paul, in life, these things happen. We often lose the ones we love," Pastor Dennis Jr. told him as they walked. "My mother was buried right there." He pointed to a nicely constructed, painted, elevated tombstone. "It was very hard for all of us. It took me a long time to finally accept that she was gone. She was the leader in our household, and her death destabilized us for some time. I could hardly stand at a pulpit and deliver a sermon. I would wake up hoping that her death was just a nightmare. It was a time in my life when I had to apply comforting scriptures and accept and believe that God could make a way in any circumstance. It was surreal; it was surreal."

Paul stood at a distance and watched as his father was buried. He noticed that he was lowered six feet under the hot earth. Paul acknowledged the manner in which they cemented the opening of the tomb and left it to dry.

He saw Barius standing a few yards away, conversing with his companions. He didn't know what they were talking about and didn't care. He gave them one last inspection, and then he was escorted to his aunt's house. He could not go back to the room that he had loved and cherished seven years earlier because it now was in the possession of people who despised him. His mother had left it all. All of the wealth that she had accumulated while she resided in Haiti was buried with Antoine. She wanted nothing to do with it. Antoine had not listened to her, and now she had taken it upon herself to solely raise her children. Antoine's death had initiated an eternal separation. Paul wanted nothing to do with his extended family on his paternal side. The end of their relationship had come.

He packed all of his clothes, making sure he left nothing behind. He counted his socks, his undergarments, his shirts, and everything else. He made sure everything was there and then locked his luggage. He went out to the corridor and noticed Ms. Augustine approaching. She had been someone Paul met many years prior. She was very honest and spiritual. He respected her in many ways. His mom also had grown fond of her. He ran toward her and gave her a welcoming hug. He loved this lady very much. She was a servant of the most-high God, whom she highly esteemed.

"Can you pray for me, Ms. Augustine?" he humbly asked.

"Sure, Paul, for what?"

"I would like to be more connected with God," Paul answered.

"Very well," she said, and she proceeded with an intercession. Her prayer was quite unique, and it felt very spiritual. At the conclusion, Paul thanked her.

"You're welcome, Paul," she said. "I tried to come to the funeral, but I could not find the correct church. I spent the whole day searching until I was finally able to come here."

"It's all right," Paul said. "Everything went quite well. The event went according to plan."

After Ms. Augustine and her friend left, Jordan came to the house with his mom, Aunt Ransel. Paul had always liked Jordan; he was one of his best friends while he was in Haiti.

"Hey, Paul, how are you doing brother?" Jordan said, greeting him with a sincere smile.

"I am doing quite well, my cousin."

"The world we live in is strange," he said. He pulled a face to show disapproval of the condition of the world. "You know, in families, many people act weird toward one another. We find that sisters act wrongly toward each other, and brothers do similar acts. There is a lack of sincerity toward each other. Families get torn apart. Those you think are for you are actually against you. There is a lack of love and a desire for self-satisfaction. People only care for themselves."

Paul could tell Jordan was trying to give him a message, but he could not speak clearly because his mom was seven yards away. Paul understood his words, however, as they were a confirmation of what Paul already knew. They validated that his father was murdered by his own family—a family that he had worked hard for all of his life, a family that he had struggled to provide for so that society would not criticize them.

"It happens," Paul said.

"You know, Paul, when I first saw your dad after he came back, I did not know who he was. It was when I heard his soft voice that I realized it was him. I was shaken, Paul. I was shaken. I did not want to believe that he had deteriorated to such an extent. His body was frail, and his face was almost completely disfigured. He lay under the sheets like a corpse. It was an unbearable sight, Paul; it was unbearable." In the next moment, he said, "I want to pursue a career in dancing."

Paul thought he had changed the conversation because the topic had been too sad. Jordan had genuinely loved his uncle Antoine, and he was very sad that he died the way he did.

"I must go," Jordan said in a voice that Paul could barely hear. It was shaky and engulfed in profound agony.

"It will be all right. God will take care of everything," Paul reassured him.

With all of the arrangements taken care of, Uncle Charles came to bring them to Port-au-Prince. On the road, they all spoke of Haiti's lack of security. Paul became anxious as he thought of the many attacks made on civilians in broad daylight by vagabonds.

"We must stop," Uncle Charles said. "I have to use the restroom"

"There's no restroom here," Paul said.

"Yes, there is; you'll see." He stopped the car and ran between some fig trees. He hid behind a bush that prevented his being seen and excreted his waste.

That is so disgusting, Paul thought. He did not dare say that out loud. He did not want his uncle to get mad at him.

They then decided they needed some food supplies. The stopped at a shop that resembled a retail store. Motorcycles were parked in front of it, and two men with guns stood in front of the doors. They seemed to inspect every corner of the perimeter with their eyes. The had a serious countenance that seemed impossible to shake. As the doors opened, the guards' eyes thoroughly inspected them.

"We must hurry, Uncle. I feel very uncomfortable here," Paul said.

"It's all right, Paul. They are here for security; everything will be fine."

"OK," he said, but his tone indicated disagreement. He walked with his uncle to the appropriate department and watched his uncle choose cooking oil. After that, he went to another department to buy another product that he needed. In the meantime, Paul went to look at the motorcycles. He remembered the red-and-white one that his dad would drive to bring him to school. He recalled the accidents he'd had on that motorcycle. One time, the chain had ground through his shoes and destroyed some of his flesh. He had to be hospitalized for some time. He remembered the many immunizations he'd had to receive. Still, there were good moments when he would be behind his dad, enjoying the breeze that blew on his face.

He looked at the price and noticed they were quite cheap, relative to the US dollar. *Maybe one day, I will purchase one*, Paul thought.

"I'm ready to go, Paul," his uncle called to him.

Paul approached the cashier and saw his uncle in the line. He stood very closely to him and waited for the cashier to serve them. When the customer in front of them had finished, the cashier checked out his uncle.

"That will be fifteen hundred gourdes," she said.

That's crazy, Paul thought. *The supplies should not cost that much.*

As if reading his mind, the cashier said, "That's the market value."

She was right, and Paul knew it. The tax on these products was the reason for their high prices.

His uncle did not argue; he took the money from his leather wallet and paid for the goods. "Thank you," he said. He knew the system. He resided in Haiti and understood that consumer goods had to be at that price for there to be any profit for the sellers.

As they got on the road to reach the capital city, Paul began to worry that hijackers might abduct them. There were many cars on the road, and it was broad daylight, so Paul hoped that no one would attempt such a feat.

The rest of the trip was quite peaceful. The struggle and battle that Paul had undergone was now over. His uncle brought other matters to his attention, and Paul listened. He tried to dismiss the fact that he had lost a significant being in his life—one he'd had hope in, one that he'd loved, and one he'd cared for.

CHAPTER 23

PAUL'S PHILOSOPHY

Men are unwise. They are susceptible to things they do not understand. Men are limited. They make promises that they cannot keep. They cannot guarantee their tomorrows. They make the wrong decisions. Men hurt men.

As Paul sat on the plane, he reflected on his philosophy. He thought about the beliefs that had structured his life. He considered them his protocols. He viewed them as the discipline that would prevent him from faltering.

One must never trust in men. They are finite. They are limited, he thought. Then he proceeded to thank God for his omnipotence, for the love God had bestowed upon him, and for continually being faithful to him. He reflected on the many days that God had consoled him with the scriptures. He could not curse God for the misfortune; rather, he felt compelled to give him praise. After all, all things worked together for the good of those who loved God.

With these last thoughts, he drifted into a peaceful sleep.

"Paul, we have arrived," his mother said as she tried to wake him.

He glanced to his right and saw a passenger unfastening her seatbelt. Looking out the window, he saw the planes that had not been boarded. He didn't know what time it was, so he turned on his mother's phone and saw that it was 6:55 p.m. They had arrived early. They were now back in the land that he loved dearly. As all of his senses returned to him, he heard many of the passengers clapping for their successful flight.

He felt a change in his character, in his perspective on life, and in his understanding of human beings.

Eager to get off the plane, he made his way to the middle aisle and reached up for his luggage. It was smaller, and he was able to take it first. After handing it to Margaret, he took the large black luggage that was hers, although it held most of his accessories.

Eager to get home, he got in line and noticed the bright smile of the flight attendant as she facilitated the exiting process. When he reached her, he gave her a cordial nod. Normally, he would have smiled, but at that very moment, he realized he had lost his smile. He picked up his gait and followed Margaret to the processing booth.

As he waited, he began to think of what lay ahead for the future. He imagined the many days that his sister would no longer say the word *dad*. He felt the most sorrow for her. He was not sure about how she would cope with Antoine's death. That was Paul's profound concern. "She will be all right," he reassured himself. As usual, he filled his mind with positive thoughts. He preferred solving situations that caused distress at the time they occurred. He was not responsible for the future; therefore, he did not feel compelled to address any misfortune it might bring. He believed that tomorrow would take care of itself.

After they had finished checking out of the airport, they made their way to the exit.

"Valeria will be here soon," his mother told him as he paced back and forth by the airport's exit doors. Grandpa Pradere had made arrangements for Valeria to retrieve them. Paul was not familiar with how punctual Valeria was, but he hoped that she would arrive soon.

With his head looking at the ground, he heard a car approaching their area. It was Valeria with her husband. As Paul began to drag his luggage toward the car, Mr. Burdeau greeted them and helped with the luggage.

In the car, the conversations were purposely focused on matters apart from the Antoine's death. Margaret spoke of how happy she'd been to see her old friends.

"Weren't you happy to see Ms. Claudia," Margaret asked Paul.

"Yes, Mother," he replied with a nod as he leaned on the car window. He understood that she needed reassurance. It was a difficult time for his mother. He understood that and wanted to help her.

The car arrived at their stop within forty-five minutes. A sense of happiness returned, as the longer the drive had taken, the more suppressed that happiness had become. This was a troublesome time when the smiles ceased.

On the Tuesday after Paul's return, he noticed the students in his French class had sorrowful expressions and were quiet that day. It was unusual. He greeted his cousin and could see that his head was down. Everyone gave Paul friendly pats on the back and asked him if he was all right. Paul assumed that his cousin had informed them about his family circumstance, and he nodded.

At school later that week, he felt fatigued and asked the teacher if he could lie down on one of the medical beds. These were in the classroom and the teacher oftentimes used them to facilitate her medical teaching.

As he lay down, he crossed his arms over his chest in a manner that resembled his father's pose in the casket. At the time, he was not conscious of his action.

"Why are you lying like someone who has died?" Lydian inquired as she walked near to where he lay.

"I don't know," Paul responded. He didn't want to describe the experience to her. Paul could see she wanted a reason for his actions, but his silence signaled to Lydian that he was not in the mood for a conversation.

Lydian walked away and became involved in a conversation with her other friends.

Seeing that, Paul rested in his state of perfect bliss—without a smile on his face.

Printed in the United States
by Baker & Taylor Publisher Services